BOOKS BY JOHN BALL

Johnny GET YOUR GUN

a novel **by JOHN BALL**

JOHNNY
GET
YOUR
GUN

 LITTLE, BROWN AND COMPANY
Boston • *Toronto*

LIBRARY OF CONGRESS CATALOG CARD NO. 71-79361

00840 11 N2

SEVENTH PRINTING

*Published simultaneously in Canada
by Little, Brown & Company (Canada) Limited*

PRINTED IN THE UNITED STATES OF AMERICA

For

Charles and Pauline Bures

Author's Note

This book was made possible through the invaluable help of the Pasadena Police Department. Thanks are due, and are tendered, to Chief Samuel Addis, Assistant Chief Carl Lindholm, Sergeant Larry Harnois, and to Virgil Tibbs's fellow investigators, James Larsch and Dallas Perkins. All of these gentlemen devoted much of their valuable time to helping with the preparation of the manuscript.

The California Angels baseball club was also more than generous in lending support. Mr. Cedric Tallis, in particular, extended himself in a hundred different ways before he was called to the general managership of the new Kansas City club. Mr. Emmett Ashford, the noted umpire, gave expert advice, as did many of the team's outstanding stars.

Finally, the author would like to express his special gratitude to the chairman of the board of the Angels, Mr. Gene Autry. This distinguished executive and philanthropist has been, and is, the idol of millions of Western fans. They couldn't have picked a better man.

John Ball

Johnny GET YOUR GUN

1

It was close to the summer solstice, so that all day long the sun had hung high in what had been a cloudless sky. Throughout Southern California, in spite of approaching evening, the heat was still thick in the air. The morning smog had been long since carried away by the Santa Ana wind so that the mountains surrounding the Los Angeles basin stood out with sharp and brilliant clarity. Because there was still no real rapid transit in any part of the city, the rush hour traffic clogged the freeways almost to a standstill. As they sat and sweltered, the motorists could look up and see the early-rising moon three quarters full in the sky.

In common with uncounted thousands of other housewives in the vast metropolitan area Maggie McGuire was making iced tea to serve with the dinner she had prepared.

At one time she had been called Margaret, but in the section of Tennessee where she had grown up very little attention was paid to formalities. As a consequence she had been dubbed Maggie well before she had started in school and Maggie she had remained during the almost forgotten days of her formal education. Now on this hot and oppressive evening, she was far from the home in which she had grown up, not yet adjusted to her new scheme of living, and Maggie still. Mike, her husband, never addressed her in any other way.

She moved about mechanically in the cramped kitchen of the little apartment. They had rented the place when they had arrived here because it had two bedrooms and was still within the price which they had felt they could afford to pay. To Maggie calling the little cubicles which had been provided "bedrooms" was a misuse of the word. They were both so small that each could hold a double bed and little else. The bed in her young son's room was a single, which allowed him to have a cheap little dresser and a wobbly table which held a confused pile of his boyhood treasures.

Maggie glanced at the clock. Mike would be home shortly and she hoped, as always, that he would be in a good mood. She had no special reason to expect trouble, but she never knew. Their venture in coming out to California, undertaken with such hope and aspirations, was not starting out well. Perhaps they had expected too much too soon, but she had noted that for the past three weeks Mike had seemed to be coming steadily closer to the raw edge of discontent.

4

Her own life had molded itself into a pattern of preparing food, looking after clothes, accommodating herself to her husband's sexual wishes, and looking after Johnny. She loved her son almost desperately, despite the fact that lately Mike had seen in her boy a smaller fragment of himself and had all but taken him over.

Through the thin wall she could hear that Johnny, in his room, was listening to the ball game on his little Japanese transistor radio. It had been the only gift they had been able to manage for him on his ninth birthday, three weeks before. Already he seemed old enough to understand that for unstated reasons they had less money to spend, as a family, than did some of the other people who lived around them.

When the single door to the apartment swung open and Mike came in almost quietly, Maggie's breath tightened, for that was not a good sign. She eased as he kissed her perfunctorily on the forehead, giving proof that he was not displeased with her. She watched as he checked the two dishes she had on the small stove to see what was being prepared for his dinner, then he went into the nine by eleven living room and sat down on the vinyl-covered settee.

Maggie recognized his mood: in some way he had been humiliated and that was one thing which Mike could not stand. As she had many times before, she reminded herself that he was a proud man. "Proud" was a good word, a respected word, far removed from such terms as "ill-tempered," "abrupt," or even "mean." Mike was none of these things; someone had once told her that he was strong-willed. That was it, strong-willed, a man not easily defeated. She preferred to think of him in that way.

She served up the simple dinner and called her men. Mike reappeared and seated himself before the kitchen table, which was one of the supplied furnishings. Johnny slid into his place with caution, aware at once that his father was not in his most congenial mood. For several strained minutes the three of them ate quietly, Maggie and her son waiting for the moment when it would please the head of the family to speak.

When it came, it was without preamble. "I got a traffic ticket today. It'll probably cost us some money."

Johnny knew instantly that whatever had occurred, his father had been in the right, nothing else was possible. Maggie kept control over the expression on her face and waited to hear the details this time.

"I was comin' up the freeway," Mike said, talking with his mouth half full and making his words deliberately harsh. "A goddamned kid in a hot rod cut in ahead of me, almost knocked my fender off."

"Mike, Johnny's here," Maggie warned cautiously.

"I know, but he's goin' to be a man and he might as well learn man's language now."

"Did you fix him, Dad?" Johnny asked eagerly.

Mike nodded. "Of course the cops didn't see him do that, they never do. I caught up with him about a mile after that, then I cut him off just like he done me. To teach him a lesson."

6

"Good!" Johnny enthused, his eyes aglow at his father's triumph.

Mike ignored the comment. " 'Course this time there was a cop on a motorbike sitting up on the bridge. He came down and gave me a ticket."

"You won't lose your license, will you?" Maggie asked. "They've got some law, I think, about how many tickets you can get. Something like that."

"Hell no, I won't lose my license!" Mike barked. That settled it and the subject was closed.

The rest of the meal was quiet and edgy. The citation would cost at least thirteen dollars, possibly as much as twenty, which meant that something would have to be given up. Johnny badly needed a new jacket, his old one was out at the elbows. Maggie decided that if he could wear it just a little longer, the money she had put aside for a new one might help to take care of the fine.

When the last of the meal was being eaten, and Johnny was industriously scraping his plate with the edge of his fork to capture the last bits of gravy, Mike turned to his son. "Johnny, I know that I promised to take you to the ball game. We'll still go, but it might have to be a little later on. Is that all right with you?"

Into Johnny's eyes tears came very quickly; he blinked rapidly several times to make them go away. He had been counting the days, and the hours, until the promised trip to Anaheim to see the Angels — Gene Autry's team. Postponing that was almost more than he could bear, but he tried, as best he could, to measure up to his father's strength of character.

"You had to do it, Dad," he said. "An' I'm real sorry about the cop." One small consolation appeared and he seized at it. "I can listen to the games on my new radio."

Mike gave his son a powerful squeeze. He did not have many moments of softness, but he realized how much it was costing his son to support what he had done. For a second he was almost ashamed of himself, then he remembered that it had not been his fault that the cop had been there.

"Can we go — some other time?" Johnny asked in a small voice.

"You bet we can. There'll be another double header. Not with the Twins, maybe, but some other good team. Maybe Boston or the Tigers. We'll go and sit in reserved seats."

There was a pause during which Mike silently cursed the policeman who had put him in this humiliating position and who was causing his son this hurt. He looked at his boy once more.

"Are you cryin'?" he demanded.

Johnny wiped his eyes with his sleeve. "I was just thinkin' about the guy who tried to hurt you," he invented to hide his shame. "And the goddamn cop."

"That's right," Mike responded. "The goddamned cop."

There was a union at that moment, an understanding

8

between father and son. "Kid," Mike said. "It's tough sometimes, but if you want to get along in this world, and be
respected, remember not to take anythin' from nobody. You're
a good clean white boy and you don't have to. You're as
good as anyone, see?"

Johnny absorbed this thoughtfully, noting the silence
of his mother. "Dad, how come Willie Mays is a — " He could
not say the distasteful word in speaking of one so great. "How
come he isn't white?"

Mike had no real answer to that question. "Because
he wasn't born that way, I guess," he said a little roughly.
"But don't worry your head about that, just remember what
I told you." He nodded to indicate that he was finished.

Johnny rose and walked into his room, thoughtfully
pondering his father's advice. He shut the door and turned
on his radio. In the scant weeks that he and his parents had
been here he had made few acquaintances and no friends;
in his lonesome little life the radio had opened the door to a
magnificent new world. People played music for him to listen
to and they told him, play by play, what was happening in
the big league baseball games. Seated on the edge of his bed
he clutched the little set in both hands and reveled in its
magic.

In the morning, when he left for school, he carefully
bunched his jacket with his hand to hide the rectangular shape
in his pocket.

His mother took no particular notice of him when

he was ready to go out the door, instead she was thinking that as soon as he had left she would be able to sit down with a cigarette and a cup of coffee to compose herself.

Her nerves were on edge. During breakfast Mike had rehashed the matter of the traffic ticket and it had only underlined things. She did not like the place where they were living, there was no joy for her in her marriage, and matters never seemed to get any better. When she heard Johnny's "Good-bye, Mommy," she said something automatic in reply and then resigned herself to the routine day ahead.

With the tingling sensation of a secret known to himself alone, Johnny got on the school bus and took his usual seat. He hardly seemed to be aware of the familiar ride. It was so seldom that he had something of which to be proud, anything new to wear, or any accomplishment to describe with glowing satisfaction at home.

The usually dull forenoon took on a new keenness as the lunch hour approached. When the bell at last rang, he ran to the cafeteria area to open his little bag of food and enjoy the incomparable luxury of eating in the company of the unseen broadcasters who would be there the moment that he clicked the switch and brought his radio into throbbing life.

As soon as he was seated he pulled out his little set and turned it on. A blast of rock and roll music answered him; he turned the dial until he heard something he liked. The music lifted his thoughts as he ate his sandwich and he thrilled to the joy of possession.

He had almost finished eating when Billy Hotchkiss, from nowhere, snatched the radio away. He took full advantage of the fact that he was two years older and considerably the larger; with the skill of a born prankster he held the set on his hand just out of reach and dared Johnny to try for it.

In that instant Johnny's world was frozen. With a noise in his throat he stretched out both his hands, trying to reclaim his set and unconsciously imploring its return. Every minute lost was something he was missing, something that was almost the key to life itself.

Billy danced away, a mocking smile on his lips. "Come and get it," he invited. As Johnny jumped to his feet, his meal forgotten, Billy began to run. Because of his size he could run much faster, and even with the urgency of desperation Johnny could not catch him. Every few moments Billy slowed down, then when Johnny could almost touch him he sprang away again, waving his hand with the radio in it over his head. Then he tossed it into the air and caught it.

The bell rang. That was a blessed relief, the lunchtime game was over and Billy would hand back the radio. He had done a cruel thing and Johnny would not forgive him for a long, long time.

"Hurry up back or you'll be late," Billy warned. Then standing on tiptoe he pushed the radio up onto a high window ledge where Johnny could not possibly reach it. "Be good," Billy said, "and I'll get it down for you after school. Now run!"

In blind, frustrated rage, Johnny lowered his head and charged his tormentor, his fists flying. Billy sidestepped expertly and slapped Johnny neatly on the side of the face. Johnny attacked again, with desperate intensity, but Billy only blocked his blows. He laughed at the huge success of his joke played on the much smaller boy who wore funny clothes and talked in such a peculiar way. He had meant to give back the radio, but his teasing had borne wonderful fruit and he didn't want to surrender such rich fun.

The final bell rang, the one which would have to be obeyed. Billy took to his heels and left Johnny alone, it was the easiest way to keep things as they were. Johnny tried once to reach his precious set, saw that it was impossible, and vowed revenge.

During the two hours of the afternoon school session he sat at his desk, his lips together, a hard look in his eyes. When at last he was released for the day, he ran back to where his radio was, determined to ask the first person tall enough to do so to reach it down for him.

Once the radio was safely back in his own hands the crisis would be over, but the agony of it would not cease until that moment. He could see the edge of his precious set protruding over the sill — proof at least that it was still there.

Billy appeared beside him. "So you want your radio, huh?" he mocked. "Well, why don't you reach up and get it."

Johnny gritted his teeth together. "Give me my radio!" he demanded.

Billy laughed. "Now you're not going to get anything

asking like that." He reached up and touched the set, emphasizing his ability to do what Johnny could not.

Johnny looked quickly around him for help, but the playground was almost empty. School was over and the children were rapidly leaving. All of the fury which he had been holding down during the bitter afternoon seized hold of him; without warning he lashed out. He caught Billy by surprise, his right fist landed on the older boy's cheek. For a moment Billy was stunned, then he swung his arms out and knocked Johnny down. Stretching up, he pulled down the radio and held it as if to dash it on the ground.

Johnny was on his feet, the knee of his trousers split, ready to fight to the death. Billy sensed that the joke had gone too far; he gulped air, sped a few feet away and when he had enough distance turned and threw the radio. He hadn't meant to do that, but he had been struck on the face and he was angry. As soon as the set was in the air he saw that Johnny wouldn't be able to catch it.

With one desperate lunge Johnny hurled himself toward the point where the radio would fall. It brushed the ends of his frantic fingers, dribbled off, and fell to the asphalt surfacing.

Billy came from where he was standing, when Johnny did not move he ventured a step or two nearer to him. From there he could see that the case was cracked.

"Gee, Johnny, I'm sorry," he offered. His anger was gone in the cold reality of guilt.

Johnny did not hear him. With a sob racking his throat,

he bent over and tenderly picked up the little plastic case that only seconds before had been to him a living thing, the best friend he had.

As he held it in his fingers he could sense that something was loose inside. With his lips quivering he very carefully clicked the switch that was supposed to turn it on. He rolled the little wheel as far as it would go towards full volume, but there was no answering sound.

Johnny cried. He did not feel the contrite hand that Billy laid on his shoulder or hear the words. "I'm sorry. My dad'll get you a new one." He was in a paroxysm of grief so all-engulfing he was alone on another plane belonging to a different world.

The thing he had loved and that had loved him was dead. The only thing he had had to cherish as his very own had been snatched from him.

By a murderer.

Billy had seized his radio, tortured it, and then hurled it to its helpless death.

His emotion changed. Total grief began to give way to blinding red anger. In awful rage his body tightened so that he could hardly breathe. Then the lust for violent revenge seized complete control of him, a great sob escaped him, and his fingers locked fiercely around the broken case of his beloved, trusted, murdered companion.

With frozen, terrible detachment he saw that for what Billy had done, Billy would have to pay. An obsession took hold of him, a total determination to do as he had been taught.

Billy was too big for him in a fist fight. He could run faster, he was stronger, and he had much longer arms. But there was another remedy that would still Billy's mocking laughter, a way to make him pay, and pay completely, for what he had done. He could have his revenge and have back his shattered honor, because he knew where his father kept his gun.

2

Estelle Hotchkiss was disturbed about her son.

He had seemed all right when he had returned from school, but he had been quieter than usual and when she had spoken to him, he had replied only in monosyllables. She had at first dismissed this as another manifestation of the kaleidoscopic moods of a growing boy.

Later on the phone had rung. Billy had answered it and had had a short conversation; when she had seen him shortly after that he had appeared to be downright terrified.

"Is there anything wrong?" she had asked. He had answered something under his breath and she had let it pass, he was often that way when he had suffered a minor setback of one kind or another. He was having trouble with history and he had mentioned that there was going to be a test on the Revolutionary War or some such topic. That, she decided, was probably it — he knew that he had done badly on the examination and it was preying on his mind.

It was good for him to worry a little, it might inspire him to study a little harder the next time.

By five o'clock Billy's odd mood had not passed, if anything it had deepened. By now Estelle had decided that something more than just an examination had gone wrong and that her son would tell her about it in his own good time. She went quietly about her normal affairs and waited for the moment to arrive.

The first real indication came when she said to him, "Billy, go outside and see if the paper has come, will you?"

"I don't want to." It was an abrupt, unusual answer.

She stopped the work she was doing and looked at him. "Billy, I asked you nicely to go and see if the paper is here, now please do it."

"I can't."

Those two words caused her a sudden chill, her son had never spoken to her like that before. She put down the carrot she had been scraping, laid the tool aside, and turned to give him her full attention.

Billy stood there, not defiantly, but with his head down.

"Billy, look at me," she said.

Reluctantly he obeyed.

"Ever since you came home from school you've been acting very strangely. I know that something is wrong. I want you to tell me what it is."

After a long moment he lowered his head again and

remained silent. For a moment she thought that it was stubbornness, then she sensed that it was far more than that. She dropped down until she was sitting on her heels and he could not escape her by looking down any longer.

"I want to know what's wrong," she repeated.

After another long pause Billy answered, dragging out the words only because he had to. "I can't tell you," he said.

Estelle Hotchkiss had grown up with three brothers, one older and two younger than herself, so she had a better than average insight into the sometimes strange world of boys. "Something happened at school, didn't it," she said.

Billy hesitated for another long interval and then nodded his head.

"Did you have trouble with one of your teachers?"

"No."

From his tone, and the way in which he spoke, she concluded reluctantly that he was in some manner in the wrong, otherwise he would have been more anxious to defend himself. She pressed her lips together for a moment, thought carefully, and then looked at her boy once more.

"Is that why you can't go and bring in the paper?" she asked.

Billy's voice was barely above a whisper. "Yes," he confessed.

"Then we'll go out and bring it in together."

Suddenly he became alive; he grasped her arm with almost frantic strength and his eyes widened in terror. "No, no!" he exploded.

18

She looked at him steadily. "Billy, what have you done?"

When he did not answer she started toward the front door, almost dragging him with her.

"Don't go out there!" he shouted.

That settled it, something very serious was wrong. Her voice changed as sympathy gave way to authority. "Billy, I want you to tell me this minute what happened. If you don't I'm going to call your father on the phone. This can't go on any longer."

Billy's eyes were suddenly wet with tears and she knew that he was close to the breaking point. "I'm going to bring in the paper," she said. It had suddenly occurred to her that there was something in it that Billy was most anxious she not see. She resolved to get the paper and to at least scan every item in it. Nothing else she could think of made sense. Without saying anything she forced him to let go of her arm and started for the door.

Then it came. In a voice that she had never heard him use before Billy cried to her, "There's a boy out there with a gun and he'll shoot you!"

She gasped for breath; she whirled toward her son. "A *real* gun?" she demanded.

"Yes!" The words came in a torrent now; Billy's hands were clenched into fists as he fought to make her believe him. "I broke his radio. I didn't mean to do it, but I did. He called me up a little while ago. He told me he had his father's gun and that he was going to come here and kill me!"

There was a pause, a cold moment of frozen horror, then Estelle Hotchkiss looked carefully at her son. He was not lying, she could see that. In three quick steps she reached the telephone and dialed operator.

"Get me the police," she said, and her own voice was shaking.

The desk sergeant who took her call passed a message to radio dispatch within seconds. It went on the air at once to officers Dick Stone and Barry Rothberg who were cruising less than two miles from the Hotchkiss home; within five minutes they were ringing the bell at the front door. At the sight of their uniforms Estelle swung the door wide and with a tight voice said, "Please come in."

A painful few minutes passed while Billy reluctantly told his story, shamefaced at having to admit what he had done, terrorized by the realization of what he had begun.

As soon as he had finished Stone looked at his partner. "I'll go outside and have a look around," he said. "Suppose you stay with these people until I come back."

"I'll go," Rothberg volunteered.

Stone did not bother to answer, he loosened his side-arm in its holster and then went promptly out the front door. He paused on the flagstone entryway for a few seconds and looked about carefully, particularly at the places where someone might be concealed. Across the street there was a parklike wooded area which had been left undeveloped; Stone noted that it would offer good concealment for anyone who might want to watch the house without being seen. Keeping a careful lookout, he walked with normal speed to the patrol car and picked up the mike. Still keeping his attention focused on the area of trees and shrubs which was much too conveniently located, he reported in.

At that hour most of the members of the day staff, including the investigative and juvenile divisions, had already gone home, but there were others who remained on the job. Community disturbances, traffic problems, fires, crime, and other matters which require police action do not obligingly cease at five, in fact the coming of darkness seems to stimulate them into greater activity. Most of the night work was done in Pasadena by the uniformed division, but there were others always available to respond when they were needed.

Virgil Tibbs was at his desk because he was scheduled for a court appearance and he wanted to be absolutely sure that his preparation was complete. Fresh in his mind was a fiasco of a few weeks before when a confidence man he had spent weeks tracking down went free because he had not been formally notified of his constitutional rights. This time the accused would not be able to get off the hook on any such excuse, but his attorney would be looking for any loophole. Tibbs was determined not to provide one.

When his phone rang he picked it up, spoke his name, and then listened. Within a few seconds he began to jot notes on a pad of ruled paper which was always in a convenient position. As he wrote down the address he was given he visualized the area and the economic bracket of the people who lived there.

"I'll go right out," he said. Automatically he set aside the plans he had made for the evening; it was most unlikely that the sort of thing he had just been told about could be resolved quickly. He could not take time even to stop for a quick hamburger, when people wanted police help every minute was magnified.

Thirteen minutes later Estelle Hotchkiss heard the doorbell ring once, discreetly, and hurried to answer it. Her husband had unfortunately picked this time to be out of his office and he was late coming home, so the full burden still rested in her hands. When she swung the door open she found herself face-to-face with a Negro; this was not what she had been expecting and for a moment she was taken aback. Then she looked again and noted that he was slender, somewhere in his early thirties, and dressed in a dark-colored, lightweight summer suit of unmistakable quality.

"I'm from the Pasadena police, Mrs. Hotchkiss," he said. "My name is Tibbs."

His speech confirmed what Estelle's quick eye had already told her, that here was a well-bred person. She had no Negro friends, but she did know that there were many Negroes of superior attainment; she was prepared to accept this man in that category. "Please come in, Mr. Tibbs," she invited. The tightness was still in her voice, but she knew he would understand that.

Virgil Tibbs walked in just as a dark blue Continental swung into the driveway. The man who got out was on the right side of forty, moderately tall, and cut from the pattern which shapes the modern businessman. He glanced quickly at the police car parked before his door, at the unmarked car with the UHF antenna which was immediately behind it, then at his wife who was still framed in the doorway. He hurried quickly across the lawn.

"What . . . ?" he asked, making the single word do the work of a sentence.

"Nothing — yet," Estelle replied. She did not need to add that she wanted his help desperately — her face showed that.

When Ralph Hotchkiss came into the foyer of his home he found Virgil Tibbs standing there, quietly waiting for Estelle to explain his presence. "Billy's in trouble," she said. "This is Mr. Tibbs from the police."

Her husband looked startled and concerned. "Come in," he said, and led the way into the living room where Barry Rothberg was seated beside Billy. One glance at his boy told him that his son had done something seriously wrong. He was relieved only to see that he was apparently all right, at least he had not been run over by a car.

"Billy, this is Mr. Tibbs," Estelle said, and then realized that without thinking she had presented an adult to an eleven-year-old child. She looked toward the man who had come to help her and apologized with her eyes; Tibbs saw it and understood. Few people took the trouble to be courteous to policemen any more; his receptions in the past had ranged from simply being taken for granted to downright hostility. There had been exceptions, like the Nunn family at Sun Valley Lodge, but they were relatively few in number.

Hotchkiss waved Virgil to a chair and then sat down beside his son. He rested his arm across his boy's shoulders as a symbol of his support and then looked at Tibbs. "I take it that you're in charge," he said.

Tibbs nodded. "I only know a little of what has happened," he began, and looked at Billy. "Suppose, son, that you start at the beginning and tell your father and me the whole story. Don't leave anything out, even if you think that it's not important. I want to know about everything just as it happened, do you understand?"

Billy looked up once into his father's face in a silent plea.

"Well, there's this funny kid at school, his name's Johnny McGuire." He stopped.

"Funny in what way?" Tibbs asked.

Billy squirmed and rubbed his palms together before he replied. "Well, he's just funny. He talks kinda funny-like and his clothes are real funny too. He's got this one jacket and it's all worn out — his elbows stick out. But he still wears it all the time. And he goes right off his rocker if you kid him a little. He can't take a joke, he gets real hot right away."

"Would you say that he is quick-tempered?"

Billy hesitated. "No, I guess not exactly. He's not a bad kid, just that he can't stand being ribbed."

"Do you play with him very much? Normally is he a friend of yours?"

"No," Billy admitted. "He doesn't have any friends because he's new and he's funny — like I told you. I tease him some, I guess, because it's a lot of fun. I guess I shouldn't."

"You've teased him before, then?"

Billy nodded.

"Suppose now you tell us what happened."

Billy unfolded his story. He did not realize that the few questions he had answered had been designed to warm him up, to get him talking, he only knew that he would have to tell it all again and that now he could hold nothing back. He felt a sense of relief as he unloaded his burden. He described how he had snatched away the radio and how he had been responsible for its being broken.

"What happened then?" Tibbs prompted.

"I said I was sorry," Billy answered, "but he didn't pay any attention. He just cried over it like it was a dead dog or something, I told you he was funny. I know I took away his radio, but what's listening to the radio? Anybody can do that anytime."

"Not if he doesn't have one," Virgil pointed out. "If you wanted to hear the ball game very badly and didn't have any kind of a radio, you might be pretty unhappy about it."

"There's lots of radios," Billy countered.

Tibbs looked for a moment at Ralph Hotchkiss who nodded that he understood. At his age Billy did not have any conception of financial limitations, he had never experienced any and to him the worn-out jacket was a symbol of eccentricity.

"With Mr. Tibbs's permission I want to say something right here," Hotchkiss said. "As soon as we are through here, Billy, you and I are going out to buy a new radio for the McGuire boy. It's going to be a good one and you're going to have to pay for it out of your own money. Then together we're going to call on the McGuires. You have a very big apology to make and it's going to be tonight."

The words had the wrong effect. The boy who a moment before had been contrite and submissive was transformed; his hands tightened into fists and he drew his feet back under himself as though he wanted to leap away — to seek shelter somewhere and hide. "No!" he exploded. "You don't understand. Johnny McGuire wants to kill me!"

Ralph Hotchkiss tightened his arm across his son's shoulders. "Take it easy, Billy," he cautioned. "You're getting much too excited. How old did you say that Johnny McGuire is?"

"Nine, maybe . . ."

"All right then, he's a little boy — smaller than you are, you said that yourself. I don't think that we need to worry too much about his trying to do something desperate."

Billy grew icy cold and made a determined effort to be believed. "Dad, you don't understand. Johnny's father's got a gun, he keeps it loaded in the house."

Hotchkiss looked quickly at Tibbs. The officer nodded

his head grimly. "It's very common," he said. "We advise citizens to register their guns for their own protection, but the great majority don't bother. There are hundreds of accidental shootings every year. And a lot more that aren't accidental."

"By children?" Hotchkiss asked, incredulity in his voice.

"Normally no, but an angry or badly upset child who has access to a loaded gun . . ." The sentence hung in the air.

Quietly and calmly Virgil Tibbs continued the thread of the interrogation. "Billy, I want to ask you two or three things and I want you to answer me as carefully and as accurately as you can, do you understand?"

"Yes, sir."

Tibbs knew then that the persistent barrier which his race often imposed in his work was not present here. He went on, simply a plainclothes policeman talking to a very upset young boy.

"Have you ever been to Johnny McGuire's home?"

"No. He doesn't have a home; they live in an apartment."

"How do you know that?"

"I don't know. I just know, that's all."

"Does Johnny know where you live?"

"Yes." Virgil detected a downward inflection and took note of it.

"Has he ever been here?"

"Once." The tinge of guilt was still present.

"Did you invite him over?"

"Yes." It was more pronounced now.

"This is very important, Billy, and I want you to give me a truthful answer, do you understand?"

"Yes, sir."

"Why did you invite Johnny McGuire to come here?"

Billy hesitated and then shrugged his shoulders. "I don't know. I just invited him."

"A little while ago you told me that he hadn't any friends because he was 'funny,'" Virgil said, speaking very clearly. "You implied, if you know what that word means, that you didn't want to be his friend either, for the same reason. Yet you invited him to your home."

Dead silence.

Tibbs waited until the full meaning had sunk in, then he continued with calculated quiet and clarity. "Billy, you have a very beautiful home here — a much better than average home. You realize that, don't you?"

"Yes, sir." The boy knew that he had been trapped.

"Did you bring him here just to tease him a little — to show him how much better your home was than the place where he lives?"

Billy's answer was barely above a whisper. "Yes."

Ralph Hotchkiss stirred in his seat, but was wise enough this time to remain silent.

"Billy," Tibbs looked at him steadily, "did you ever try to be a friend to Johnny McGuire? Any time at all?"

"I guess not."

Tibbs eased the pressure. "That's all right, there's no reason why you should if you didn't want to. It's your privilege to choose your own friends. But Johnny McGuire has been here and does know where you live."

"Yes, I remember now — when he was here he said that there's only one bathroom in his apartment. That's how I found out about that."

"Good, I'm glad that you remembered. Now why do you think that you are in physical danger from Johnny McGuire?"

Billy responded to the letup in pressure as Virgil had intended he should. He felt that he could talk and be believed.

"Johnny called me up on the phone. I don't know how he got the number, but he called. Then he said a funny thing — he said that I had killed his radio. That's what he said, 'killed.' Then he said that he was going to kill me."

"A lot of children say things like that."

Billy lifted his face and revealed that tears were beginning to roll down his cheeks. "But he means it, Mr. Tibbs. He told me that he was coming to get me."

He stopped to be sure that everyone understood.

"He said that he was going to kill me." The tears came now in a torrent. "He said that he had taken his father's gun, and that he had it with him."

29

3

Virgil Tibbs knew, to his sorrow, that such a thing was entirely possible. He hoped fervently that it was not the case this time, but he could not afford to take any chances. "May I use the phone?" he asked.

"Of course," Hotchkiss answered him. "If you would like privacy, there's an extension in my den." He got quickly to his feet, showed him the way, and then carefully closed the door of the study behind him as he left.

The atmosphere in the living room remained still and tense until Virgil reappeared. "I've made some arrangements," he announced. "Officer Rothberg is going to remain here with you for a little while if you don't mind. I think it's desirable."

"So do I," Hotchkiss agreed.

"After I find out where he lives I'm going over to see

the McGuire boy; it's getting close to the dinner hour and I expect that will bring him home. As soon as I have any definite information, I'll phone you here."

"Let me give you the number," Hotchkiss volunteered, reaching for his wallet.

"I already have it, thank you. Officer Rothberg will be responsible in the meantime; I suggest that you follow any instructions that he may give you."

"We will," Estelle Hotchkiss promised.

When Mike McGuire arrived home that evening he was in a dark and silent mood. He disappeared into the bathroom briefly and then returned to sit wrapped in his own thoughts in the small living room. When his wife came to tell him that his dinner was ready and waiting, he responded mechanically. As she set his plate in front of him he did not even appear to see his food. "Where's Johnny?" he asked.

"He went out to play," Maggie answered. "He hasn't come back yet."

The two of them sat down to the business of eating, but there was no sense of companionship and no attempt at conversation. Maggie had no idea what might be wrong, but ten years of marriage to this man had taught her not to probe. She waited several minutes for him to break the silence. "I don't like the kid bein' out like this," he said at last. "He oughta be home eatin' his dinner."

"He can't be long," Maggie said. "He's usually always here when he should be."

"He come home from school all right?" Mike asked.

She nodded. "He stayed a little while and then went out again."

"What did he say?"

"Nothing."

Mike pondered for a moment. "Probably the Angels lost. He's nuts about that ball team."

It was almost an insult to tell her that, as though she did not know the first thing about her own child. She opened her mouth to say something and then quickly shut it again when she saw that her husband was about to speak once more. When he did, his tone was low.

"I went down this noon to pay that ticket that I got. Well, Maggie, it ain't so good; the cop put me down for reckless driving and I've got to go to court. The boss belongs to the motor club so I called them and they said that it could cost as much as five hundred dollars."

Maggie's breath stopped dead in her throat.

"Mike!" she gasped.

"I know," her husband answered. "It was my damn foul luck that that cop was up on the bridge and saw me. He didn't see the other guy of course, when he did what he did — they never do. Anyhow his car hit the divider, I didn't know that, and it was bent up some."

"Will we have to pay for that too?"

"We've got insurance." Awkwardly he reached out and took her hand, something he had not done in years. "I'm gonna tell the judge that I thought the fellow in the lane to my left was goin' to pull over and that I moved to get out of his way. That may help."

"Will he believe you?"

"He might. Anyhow, I can't go to court and admit I was just after that guy's scalp. You know what that would mean."

"Mike, if he doesn't believe you, what'll we do? You'd have to sell the car, then how'd you get to work?"

There was silence for several seconds. "I'll go to a loan company," he answered finally. "Maybe you could get something to do, part time while Johnny's in school. For long enough to pay back the loan, that's all."

Maggie blinked, she had no skills she could use to get a job. All she had to offer was herself and besides, Johnny came home just a little after three.

Johnny.

They both remembered at the same moment. "He oughta be here," Mike declared, as though by the statement he could make him appear.

Maggie got up, opened the outside door, and remained there for a long minute. When she turned back, her face was lined with anxiety. She said nothing, because there was nothing to say.

"He might be asleep in his room." Mike spoke quickly, then led the way for the few steps to Johnny's little sanctuary. He was not there. His bed was smooth and undisturbed, just as Maggie had made it for him that morning. They both stood and looked at the narrow empty bed.

"Is his radio there?" Mike asked.

Maggie did not have to search for long to determine that it was gone. While she was looking she came across his little strongbox, which was actually made of light metal and held shut with a toy lock. She left it strictly alone because it held a secret which she shared with her son.

Mike turned toward the other bedroom. He swung the door open quickly, took one look, and saw that it too was empty. He smothered his disappointment with the thought that if his son had been asleep it would have been in his own room. But it had been worth a look.

Then he thought about kidnappers. They picked up children, sometimes without any knowledge of who their parents were or how much they might be able to raise to get them back. Another idea hit him: Johnny was nine now and there were people who were looking for young boys of just about that age. He clamped his teeth together and for one hot instant saw himself throttling to death anyone who would attempt such a thing with *his* son. Then he forced himself to calm down and remembered that Johnny had only been gone a little more than an hour past the time when he should have been home.

He turned to his wife. "It's light now to past eight-thirty. He's forgotten about what time it is; he's probably playing baseball somewhere. Kids are like that. Let's finish dinner."

Reluctantly Maggie accepted his judgment and went

back to the kitchen where the beef stew she had prepared was now cold and congealed. "It's all right," Mike said. "I like it this way." He ate a few mouthfuls in silence, listening for the sound of footsteps on the concrete walkway outside. When he heard them he jumped, although he knew at once that it was not his son who was coming. When he heard the sound of the doorbell he was already on his feet.

He flung the door wide and found himself looking at a slender but well-built Negro who appeared to be in his early thirties.

"Well?" Mike demanded.

"My name is Tibbs," the man said. "I'm from the Pasadena police. It's very important that I talk to you and your son immediately."

"Well Johnny ain't here!" Mike blazed out the words. Then his chest tightened at the sudden thought that perhaps this black man had news to tell him. "What's happened?" he asked.

"Nothing — yet. May I come in, please?"

Mike let him in, hostility forming an aura around him. He disliked all policemen automatically, today more than usual.

Maggie looked up and saw the visitor was wearing better clothes than her husband owned. She was dubious of his color, but anxiety overrode her other feelings and she said, "Won't you sit down, please."

Virgil Tibbs seated himself quietly at the table and

then waited for Mike McGuire to calm down enough to join them.

"As far as we know now your son is all right," Virgil began. "Can you tell me when you saw him last?"

Maggie pressed the back of her hand against her forehead. "He came home this afternoon after school. He poked around a little while in his room. I didn't pay much attention; I was ironing. Then he went out again."

"Has he been out late like this before?"

"Never," Mike answered.

"Has he any close friends he might be visiting?"

Maggie unwittingly confirmed what Billy Hotchkiss had already said. "He don't really have any friends here yet. We're new."

Tibbs said, "You left Tennessee in February I assume."

Mike tightened so that the veins of his muscular forearms stood out. "You been checking up on us?" he demanded.

Virgil shook his head. "When I came in, I noticed the cars parked downstairs. There were seven — four with California plates, and one each from Canada, New Jersey, and Tennessee. Your manner of speaking suggests that the Tennessee car is yours. And most people with young children plan their moves, if they can, at the end of school terms."

Mike rubbed his fingers hard against his jaw. "I guess it's all right, I just never like to have people prying into our business."

Tibbs studied him. "I don't pry, Mr. McGuire, I'm

a police investigator and it's my business to notice things. Right now I'm trying to use what abilities I have to help you."

"I'm sorry," Mike said.

Virgil produced a notebook and opened to a clean page. "I'd like a description of Johnny," he requested. "And please tell me what he's now wearing."

Maggie responded. "Johnny has just turned nine. He's a little small for his age, but he's a nice-looking boy. His hair is still light and he has blue eyes. He's got on a pair of jeans from Penney's and his black school shoes." Then she remembered. "He has his jacket," she added a little lamely. "A red one. It's out at the elbows and we've been meaning to get him a new one."

"Do you have a picture of him?"

Maggie got up. "I'll try and find one," she said.

As soon as she had gone Mike leaned forward, enough to be heard softly, but not enough to bring him too close to the black man who was a cop in the bargain. "You think he's been kidnapped?" he asked.

Tibbs shook his head. "I'm very confident that that isn't the case, for a number of reasons."

"Such as?" Mike asked.

"If kidnappers were looking for a child to seize and hold for ransom, I doubt if they would choose one who was wearing a worn-out jacket." He could have supplied a much better reason, but he was not ready yet to disclose all that he had learned at the Hotchkiss house.

The phone rang, loudly because it was installed in the kitchen. Mike scooped it up quickly and made the word "Hello?" into a question.

"Mr. McGuire?"

"Yes, Mike McGuire speaking. Go on."

"This is Ralph Hotchkiss, Mr. McGuire, Billy's father. I've just been given your number by the police department."

"I don't want to talk about the accident now."

"Very well, but I just wanted to tell you how very sorry Billy is for what he did. If your son is there, Billy would like to talk to him."

"He ain't come home. We're worried about him."

Hotchkiss was very guarded. "Have you spoken to the police?"

"One of 'em is here now."

"Good. If I learn anything at all, I'll call you. Good night, Mr. McGuire."

As he hung up the instrument growing suspicion began to take over in the forefront of Mike's mind. He did not see his wife as she reappeared in the doorway holding a snapshot in her hand, instead he stared straight ahead while he allowed the cancer of distrust to nourish itself and grow. His jaw muscles began to work and his eyes grew hard. "I think that guy knows somethin'!" he exploded. His voice echoed back from the hard walls. He turned toward Tibbs as though expecting him to do something at once.

"Mr. McGuire," Virgil asked, "do you own a gun?"

"Yes, I've got a gun — what of it?"

"What kind of a gun?"

"A Colt thirty-eight. Why?"

Tibbs ignored the question. "Do you customarily keep it loaded?"

"What the hell good is a gun if it ain't loaded? I've got a right to have it, the Constitution says so. Don't you give me no argument on that!"

There was a moment of thick silence.

"You have the legal right to own a gun," Tibbs said. "You're asked to register it for your own protection, but you're not required even to do that."

"Then what's the gripe?"

"I didn't say that there was a gripe. Mr. McGuire, have you ever allowed your son to handle your gun?"

"Sure every kid should know how to handle a gun. He might have to protect his ma sometime when I'm not here."

"He knows, then, where you keep it?"

"Of course he does."

Virgil rose to his feet, automatically Mike did the same. That brought them face-to-face and Mike, to his surprise, read power and authority in the dark eyes opposite his.

"I'd like to see your gun, Mr. McGuire. Immediately, if you please."

Mike sensed that he would have to comply. He walked firmly past his wife, out of the kitchen, and across the small

39

living room in his role as master of the house. He paused in front of a narrow linen closet and opened the door. A moment later he turned around to find that Tibbs was behind him and waiting.

"It's gone," Mike said.

4

This time Virgil Tibbs did not wait to ask if he could use the telephone, he returned to the kitchen, picked it up without ceremony, and dialed the headquarters number.

"Tibbs at the McGuire home," he reported in. "The boy, Johnny, has not come home. Almost certainly he has his father's loaded handgun with him and he knows how to use it."

"Good God!" the desk sergeant responded. "It's true."

"Right. You'd better call the Hotchkiss home immediately and tell Barry Rothberg the score. Then set up a stakeout to cover the exterior. The boy may still come home on his own, I hope to heaven that he does, but we can't bank on it. Also run the full missing child routine — hospitals and all the rest. I'll be here for a few more minutes."

He hung up, turned, and found the McGuires where they had been standing, listening, behind him. "I don't want to upset you," he told them, "but this could develop into a very serious situation. I'm hoping that Johnny will come home by himself. If he does, I suggest that you treat him with an extra measure of consideration and love, because he will be needing it."

Maggie began softly to cry.

"I think you had both better sit down," Virgil advised. "I have some things to tell you."

The belligerency drained out of him for the moment, Mike did as directed. Maggie, her shoulders shaking, followed suit.

In quiet, calm tones Tibbs told them what had happened in the schoolyard and of Johnny's violent reaction. Then he carefully repeated Ralph Hotchkiss's offer to replace the smashed radio set at once.

Mike pondered the matter. "If this Hotchkiss will buy him a new radio, with a battery and everything, then I guess it's all right. But it was plain dirty what his kid did to Johnny, and I can't blame Johnny for getting damn mad. That smart-alec kid of Hotchkiss's needs a good whipping and maybe someday Johnny'll give it to him." As he spoke the last words the first dawn of comprehension began to show on his face. "My gun," he said, forming the words mechanically, "he took my gun."

Grimly Virgil nodded. "Yes, Mr. McGuire, he has your

gun. I think he means to use it and the Hotchkiss family is very frightened."

"Oh, my God, no!"

Maggie flung her hands over her face and bent over the table, her body shaking with sobs. Mike got up quickly and put his arm around her, to comfort her and to hide his own acute embarrassment. After the single, shattering outburst Maggie calmed down and began to sob; she had no handkerchief so Mike tore off a paper towel and handed it to her. Tibbs remained silent; when the paper towel had been used and pushed away he reached into his own pocket and produced a clean linen handkerchief which he offered to her.

She hesitated a second, then took it, wiped her eyes, and blew her nose. That finished she looked up at Tibbs. "What can we do?" she asked.

"First of all, stay here and wait for your boy to come home. If he does, tell him you've been worried, but don't upbraid him. Give him his dinner, make him glad that he came home, then please call me right away. If I'm not there, talk to the man who answers the phone." He laid a calling card on the table.

Mike indicated that they would do as directed. The realization of what might possibly happen was clear in his mind and he was very much sobered.

"Before I go, I'd like to have a little more information," Virgil said. "It could help us to find your son sooner."

"That's all right," Mike responded.

"I take it that Johnny liked his radio very much."

"It was his birthday present, he listens to it all the time. He's nuts about the Angels baseball team and he hears all the games when he ain't in school."

"Does he follow the Dodgers too?"

"No, he don't like the Dodgers, just the Angels. The Dodgers, they don't play on TV. Mostly he likes the Angels because of Gene Autry. You know about him?"

"Everybody knows about Gene Autry," Virgil answered. He stressed the first word just a little, he could not help it.

"Well, Johnny met him once. Just a quick handshake, but it was a big thing for him. Autry called him his pal and Johnny never forgot it. That was back home. Now Johnny wants to be a ball player so he can be on his team — Autry's I mean."

"Someday soon it might be a good idea to take him to a game," Tibbs suggested.

Mike was unaware of the hidden question in that simple-sounding sentence, he only knew that he felt obliged to say something in response. "I was planning to do that, but then somethin' came up. . . ."

"The accident?"

Mike looked at him with narrowed eyes. "You know about that too?"

"You mentioned it on the telephone to Mr. Hotchkiss."

Again the muscles of Mike's jaw worked. "I guess

44

maybe I did." He drew breath and let it out again very slowly.

"Could Johnny have taken any money with him?" Tibbs asked, deliberately changing the subject.

Mike shook his head. "He gets fifty cents allowance when I can spare it, but it's always all gone before the end of the week."

"No, it isn't," Maggie said.

Her husband looked at her, surprised and with a slight show of rising temper.

"It was a secret I promised to keep for him," she explained, her lower lip quivering in spite of herself. "He hardly ever spent anything. He's been saving his money for weeks to buy a catcher's outfit. He wants to be a baseball catcher. He knows we don't have much, so he's been putting it all away."

"Do you know where?" Virgil asked quietly.

Maggie nodded and led the way. Maggie ran her hand quickly across her eyes before she opened the bottom drawer of the dresser and pulled out the tin box. She was being forced to betray his little secret.

The box was not locked: Maggie opened it and handed it to Tibbs. Inside, scotch-taped to the lid, there was a newspaper photograph of Tom Satriano, the first-string catcher of the Angels, in full regalia. Otherwise it was empty.

Virgil looked at it very carefully before he handed it back. "Do you know how much he had?" he asked. "Could you hazard a guess?"

Maggie swallowed before she answered. "Sixteen dollars, maybe just a little more. I helped him out a bit when I could — for being a good boy." She glanced at her husband almost fearfully and was visibly relieved when he showed no further signs of displeasure.

"Then he's gone and taken his money with him," Mike said.

Tibbs remained silent as he studied the little room with considerable care; with nodded permission from Maggie he checked the inside of all three drawers of the inadequate dresser. When he finally did speak his voice carried a subdued, but unmistakable note of authority. "Mr. McGuire, are you in the habit of spending much time with your son?"

Mike looked at him sharply. "I do when I can."

"Then you have discussed with him what are commonly known as the facts of life?"

"As much as I thought necessary." The answer had an edge to it. "Are you sayin' that he ran away because he didn't like his old man?"

"No," Virgil answered. "My guess is that your son believes in you completely. You are probably his idol — his example for everything he does."

"It's the ball players he's nuts about," Mike retorted, but he was clearly mollified nonetheless. He was about to add something when the phone rang once more.

Mike ran to answer it, then passed the instrument to Tibbs in disappointment. "It's for you."

The conversation was brief and one-sided; after listen-

46

ing for several seconds Virgil hung up and turned to his host. "One more question, Mr. McGuire — a very important one. Have you, in your talks with your son, ever advised him what to do if others oppose him?"

Mike did not answer immediately, from the tightness of his jaw it was obvious that he was debating whether or not he would. He spoke only after he had apparently decided that he had no other choice. "I told him not to take any . . . not to let anyone boss him around."

In the thick pause that followed the hard, ugly outlines of the missing gun hung in the air.

"Mr. McGuire," Tibbs began, "you mentioned that you had planned to take your son to the baseball game and then 'something came up.' Later you referred to an accident. I've just learned that you were recently cited for reckless driving; according to the officer who saw you, you deliberately tried to force another car off the freeway and into the divider."

"Do we have to talk about that now?" Mike flared.

"Only to ask if your son knows about this matter."

"Yes, he knows. He heard me tell his mother."

Tibbs did not pursue the matter further, he had learned all that he needed to evaluate the situation which faced him. "I can relieve your minds on one point," he said. "Whenever a child is missing, no matter what the circumstances, we always make an emergency check of all the hospitals in the vicinity and other facilities. So far no one who could possibly be Johnny has been brought in."

He paused to let that much sink in.

"Since we know why he is away from home, I think we can rule out any likelihood that he's been hurt. The problem now is to find him and return him to you before he has a chance to do any damage." He did not emphasize what kind of damage he meant; they knew.

Maggie shook her head and pressed her hands across her face.

"Johnny knows how to take care of himself," Mike said.

"No, Mr. McGuire, he doesn't," Virgil retorted. "No nine-year-old boy does, he simply doesn't have the physical strength or the mental maturity to fight his way in an adult world. And the possession of a gun doesn't erase those considerations." Quietly he got up to leave. "I'm going out to look for your son," he said simply. "You know what to do if he comes back."

Mike, in control of himself once more, replied. "We'll call you."

Tibbs left quickly and shut the door behind him. Once he was outside he began an intensive search of the apartment house area. He was fully aware that children who are afraid to go home frequently huddle somewhere nearby, trying to gather courage to face their irate parents. He looked carefully inside the McGuire car and then checked the others on the parking lot. He examined every public part of the premises and then all of the likely places in the close vicinity where a young boy might elect to hide. He gave no thought to the

48

fact that the child in question was armed with a loaded gun; if he found him it would be time then to deal with that contingency.

His search was fruitless; after forty minutes he was forced to conclude that what had been a good bet had not paid off. Furthermore, the fact that Johnny McGuire was not there added to the seriousness of the problem. Normally children were quick to lose their tempers and equally quick to recover them; it would be hard for a young boy to remain enraged when he was alone in the dark of early evening and away from his home, family, and dinner. But if such were the case, then the gravity of the matter automatically increased by another damning percentage.

For the moment defeated, Tibbs got back into his official car, turned on the radio, and started for the Hotchkiss house. A thorough search in that vicinity was the next logical step. On the way he drove very slowly, watching the road only as much as was necessary. The rest of the time he gave close attention to the sidewalks, to clusters of shrubbery, and to all of the other places where a nine-year-old boy might be. He found nothing. He passed the silent schoolyard where the whole thing had happened and continued on into the better class neighborhood where the Hotchkiss home was located. He was three or four minutes away from his destination when the radio came alive with his call.

He picked up the microphone and answered.

"We've got him," the dispatcher reported. "One of the

cruise cars picked him up. About eight or nine, poorly dressed, says his name is Johnny."

"Praise God," Tibbs said. "Do the parents know yet?"

"No, wanted to check with you first."

"Then hold it, bring the boy into the station. The father is an explosive type and I'd better take the boy home myself. I'll notify the family from there. I want to find out about the gun he has — or had."

"Ten four."

Virgil U-turned and set a direct course for headquarters. He breathed a little more heavily from sheer relief; it had been a sticky one while it had lasted. A gun held by a child fires bullets which travel just as far, just as fast, as any others.

It took him twelve minutes to reach the parking lot, another three to get into the building, up the stairs to the second floor, and into the office of the juvenile division. The little boy who awaited him there turned up a tear-streaked face full of fright and despair, then he brightened just a little when he saw that the policeman coming into the room was a person like himself.

Virgil picked up the little boy, who showed unmistakable signs of some Negro blood, and comforted him across his shoulder. "We'll find your people for you right away," he promised. Then, looking toward the uniformed officer who had been waiting with the lad, he carefully shook his head from side to side.

50

The policeman left at once and hurried downstairs to the radio room. "It isn't the McGuire boy," he reported.

The dispatcher in charge reacted quickly. "Damn it, I pulled the men away from the Hotchkiss house. They're on their way in." He began to write a quick message for the duty man to put on the air.

Less than a minute later, out of the still night, a sharp explosive sound split the air and a .38 bullet crashed through the front window of Billy Hotchkiss's home to bury itself deep in the woodwork.

5

A sudden wave of fright swept through Johnny Mc-
Guire so that for a few seconds he could not move a muscle.
The gun had made an unexpectedly terrifying noise and it
had kicked in his hand like a living thing fighting to get loose.
The desperate mood which had held him for so long had
shattered with the silence when the venomous gun had gone
off.

When he had first taken it from the drawer where his
father kept it, blinding rage had possessed him; Billy's taunt-
ing face had been burned into his brain until it had eclipsed
everything else. He had carefully put the weapon into a brown
paper bag and had gained confidence from the fact that on
the street no one had given him, or what he carried, a second
glance. He had waited here in the wooded plot well out of
sight for a long time, hoping that Billy would come out of
the door of his home.

When he had seen the policemen come, and had guessed their purpose, he had simply walked away, clutching his bag in one hand. He had gone far enough to reach Colorado Boulevard where he had purchased two small hamburgers with his money and had topped them off with a thick, starchy milk shake which had come ready-mixed out of a machine. Nourished, he had gone back to find the police cars gone. For a few minutes, as the darkness had gathered, his purpose had wavered. Then recognizing the kind of weakness which his father would have despised, he had pulled out his poor, dead radio and had tried once more to turn it on. If by some miracle it had come to life, he would have broken down with tears of relief and gratitude, but the helpless smashed thing had only lain like a crushed bird in his hand and all of his rage at its destruction had come back anew.

Impatient and unable to wait any longer, he had fired the gun. He had pointed it toward the window, had held it in his two hands, and had pulled the trigger. It had shocked him with a deafening blast of sound amplified even more by the quiet of early evening. For the moment he was frozen, then, yielding to panic, he began to run. At the edge of the little park he paused only long enough to replace the gun in its paper sack, then he emerged onto the deserted sidewalk and began to hurry, as fast as he dared, toward the main artery where he had bought his dinner. He kept looking about him for some place to hide; he knew that after what he had done they would come looking for him in a hurry and he did not want to be caught.

In three minutes he reached the corner and saw, coming toward him, a city bus. One quick glance showed him a bus stop sign only a few feet away. He ran to it and waited, not caring where the bus was going so long as it would take him away from where he was.

With a snort of compressed air the big vehicle pulled up and the door opened. Johnny got on, clutching his paper bag in his left hand, while he fished with his right in his pocket for the fare. He found a quarter and brought it out. The driver accepted it as he swung away from the curb, paying no further attention to the passenger he had just taken on. The bus was more than half empty, but for maximum safety Johnny chose a seat well by himself and close enough to the front so that he could see where he was going. If the route took him close to his home, then he could find sanctuary there and his father would protect him; if it didn't then he would have to get off at some point where they wouldn't look for him.

He could not tell which direction the bus was going, only that it was not taking him home. Then, as he sat, a faint acrid odor began to reach him. In its paper bag the gun was giving off a thin, harsh smell.

To stop it he pushed the paper bag and the thing it held inside the protection of his jacket. As soon as he had done so he realized that he might have accidentally moved the trigger; fright seized him for a moment, then his wits came back and he reasoned that if he sat very still the danger would be much less.

54

Almost frozen, he did not dare to move until the bus had made several stops. After the first two no more people had gotten on, each time after that when it had pulled up to the curb someone had gotten off. When there were only three riders left besides himself he knew that they must be nearing the end of the line. He had to risk movement then; very cautiously he got up and went to the rear door. The driver went past two more corners before he stopped and let him off. A few seconds later he was alone while the taillights of the vehicle receded down the unfamiliar street.

As soon as it was far enough away Johnny very carefully brought out the package and held it in his hand. It was heavy now and he wondered if he dared to throw it away. He didn't want it any more and it was dangerous to carry. Then he thought of his father and the fury that would surely come over him if his gun were not returned in good condition. His father's anger was something he could not face; whatever happened, he would have to keep the gun.

Instinct told him that he could not stand alone on the corner too long, someone would be sure to see him and ask him what he was doing there. He wanted very much to go home, but he had no idea where he was. He thought of trying to telephone his mother, but he was in a residential sector of what was clearly a poorer class neighborhood. After what he had done he could not simply go to a house and report himself lost, he would have to try something else.

He began to walk. The best thing he could do, he decided, would be to find some place where he could hide for the night; it was early summer and with his jacket on it would not be too cold. In the morning he would walk until he found a telephone and then call his mother. She would help him.

Then behind him he heard the squeal of brakes and the sudden stopping of a car. He turned in alarm, fearful of the goddamned cops, but there were no cops there. Instead he saw a very old car which had been modified so that it was very low in front, high in the rear, and decorated with racing stripes down its side. Someone got out and called to him, "Hey, kid!"

His first impulse was to run, then he saw that the person coming toward him was only a few years older than himself. He knew that if he tried to run he could easily be caught, so he did the only possible thing and stood his ground. But he was in no mood to take chances: perhaps this person wanted to help him, perhaps not. Carefully he slid his right hand inside the top of the paper bag.

The adolescent from the car came closer and then Johnny saw that he was dark-skinned. He expected no friendship or help from such as him; he took a step or two backwards and fitted his fingers around the weapon which was now his best protection.

"Watcha got in the bag, kid, huh?" the Negro boy asked.

"My lunch," Johnny answered. It was the only thing he ever carried in such a bag and the only answer he could think to give.

56

The older boy from the car turned and called back, "Hey, get this — he says it's his lunch in the bag." He bent over in imagined silent mirth.

Johnny stepped backward once more, far enough to give himself a little distance, not so far as to invite the Negro youth to follow. Then he looked and saw three more figures getting out of the car. One of them was taller, but that was all that he could tell in the darkness.

"I'm hungry," the teen-ager in front of him said. "How about givin' me somethin' to eat, huh. Got any fried chicken?"

"It's *my* lunch," Johnny retorted.

"You're out kinda late ain't cha, kid?" Johnny recognized the change of subject as an attack from a new direction.

"I'm goin' home," he answered. "My dad's gonna meet me." He hoped that would frighten them off — if they knew his father it would.

The gambit failed. He looked up to find that he was staring at four dark Negro faces, faces that looked at him as though he were a cornered animal they could toy with for their own amusement. He would have been terrified except for one thing — the gun, the wonderful protector he held hidden in his right hand. He now saw his father's wisdom in owning it and always keeping it close, ready for immediate use. The gun might be the only thing that would save him now, a Tennessee boy, from the clear danger he saw in the four black faces.

The tall one, who seemed a little older, spoke up. "Maybe you're lost, how about that?"

"I come here all the time," Johnny flared. He did not dare to show weakness.

"Ya do, huh?" that first one said. "Then what's the name o' this street? Tell us, go ahead."

Johnny didn't know, he hadn't looked at the sign on the corner. "You leave me alone!" he demanded, putting all the thin authority he could into his voice.

"Whatcha say that for, huh? You don't like us, maybe?"

"You're niggers," Johnny responded.

One of the two remaining faces that had stayed silent until now reacted sharply. "That ain't a word we like," he said.

The tall one spoke again. "Kid, we don't like to be called that. You oughta know. You from the South?"

"Tennessee." Johnny hadn't meant to reply, but the answer was so easy he gave it.

"Well, that ain't too bad a place, but it ain't too good neither. You talk like maybe you come from Mississippi."

"Never been there," Johnny said.

"Maybe you'd like to come ridin' with us. We'll take you home."

"Don't ride with niggers," Johnny flung back. He backed away, several steps this time, and they followed him, moving the same distance that he had.

"Kid, we tol' ya not to use that word! You do it again and you got trouble!"

58

A little desperately Johnny turned and looked all around him — for someone, anyone — for a car coming by. It was strangely silent and the single streetlight was back at the corner where he had gotten off the bus.

"Let's see the bag," the first boy demanded, and grabbed for it. Johnny drew his hand back quickly; the bag came off in his tormentor's fingers and the naked gun was left exposed, pointed toward the quartet which faced him.

The fourth face spoke at last. "He's got a toy gun — look."

Johnny backed two more steps and held the gun level; he had fired it once and he could do it again. "It's no toy," he said. "It's real."

"Better give it to me."

"No."

"How come you got it? Your father's a cop, heh?"

"No," Johnny repeated.

Then silently, as though they had rehearsed it, the four dark faces separated; the tall one began to walk behind him while the two quiet ones moved to flank him on each side. Johnny froze his attention on the one still facing him in front. He was frightened, but his fear gave him a kind of coldness. He formed a quick and binding partnership with the gun in his hand; they were afraid of it, he knew, and that meant that they were afraid of him.

The boy before him tried hard to take command with his voice. "Kid, gimme that gun!"

Without thinking Johnny moved to take one more step backwards, his left foot was still in the air when he felt two sudden strong hands seize his upper arms, pinning them to his sides. The outrage of being manhandled burst the thin bubble of his self-control. He yanked hard, blindly, to get himself free — he remembered doing that, then everything disintegrated in a violent blast of sound. He knew that the gun had fired itself, it had defended him, but nothing else would take shape. The world spun around him and a hoard of demons zoomed down upon him from the sky.

The hands that had been holding him let go, they actually pushed him away. He staggered forward to keep his balance, looked and saw a human face in sudden agony and shock. The boy who had first stopped him, his hands clutched over his abdomen, was slowly sinking to the ground.

Johnny stood stock-still, looking at what the gun had done. It had not been his own doing, only the gun's — a living deadly thing.

He expected people to come running, to seize him, for the cops to pull up within seconds in their black and white cars, but the echo of the blast was stillness and the street remained as deserted as before.

Instinct seized him then; it caused him to whirl about, to take one last desperate look at the thing on the ground, and then to run harder, faster, longer than he ever had before. He saw an opening between two buildings and turned down it. It went all the way through to the next street; his heart was

60

pounding hard when he reached the end of the passageway, but terror still had complete possession of him and the stabbing pains in his chest went unheeded. He saw that the street was free except for two cars retreating the other way; he dashed across it, found another opening, and flung himself inside.

He had to rest for a few precious seconds. His heart seemed to be trying to pound its way out of his chest, but he dared not heed it in his desperation. Gulping air, he set off once more, cutting between the buildings, stopping momentarily when his body forced him to, but driving himself to the limit that his burning brain could force out of his body.

He did not know how long he went on, how many streets he crossed without being seen, but when he reached a wider and busier thoroughfare he knew that he had to stop. He looked down at his right hand and saw that he was still carrying the gun; he had not dared to throw it away. Knowing that it must not be seen, he pressed back into the shadows. His desperate flight had exhausted him. For a few seconds he did not care what happened to him, then instinct returned and he looked about quickly for a solution to his problem.

Only a few feet away there was a tall trash can without a lid. He went to it and looked inside; there was a pile of waste barely visible in the semidarkness and, jammed halfway down one side, a shoe box.

He pulled it out, took off the lid, and saw the wet and soggy body of a dead kitten. The sight turned his stomach;

in one automatic motion he dumped out the pathetic little body, sobbed, and then burst into tears as he carefully but quickly put his gun into the box and pushed it under his arm.

With the natural cunning of the pursued he went to the corner and forced himself to cross Orange Grove Avenue in a quiet and normal manner. When he reached the sanctuary of the other side he saw that there was a huge ravine ahead of him and he knew that it should give him a place to hide. He climbed down the steep slope of the Arroyo Seco in the near darkness, step by uncertain step, until he found himself at the bottom in a well-wooded part of the park.

He made his way from point to point, deeper into the gully, until he found a place where he was sure that no one would come before daylight. He crawled underneath a thick clump of bushes, heedless of the scratches being inflicted on him, and wormed his way into the center of the dense planting. There he carefully lay down, grasped the shoe box tightly in his arms, and surrendered, utterly exhausted, relaxing into a kind of stupor. Minutes later he was asleep and breathing deeply.

6

During the first few terrible seconds after the bark of the gun and the crash of the bullet through the front living room window, Ralph Hotchkiss's reaction was one of shocked disbelief. Then a burning demand for action seized him and he lunged toward the front door of his home.

He heard the word "No!" and then felt the impact as his wife flung herself in front of him. She threw her arms around his waist. "No, no!" she repeated. "Don't go, don't, he'll kill you!"

The impact of her words hit him. He quickly pulled Estelle down to the floor and pressed her shoulders there.

"Don't get up," he ordered. "Stay right there. I'll call the police." As he finished speaking the phone rang.

Holding himself bent over to make a smaller target he ran to the phone, lifted it off, and quickly said, "Yes?"

"This is Mr. Tibbs," the voice said. "We took the guard off your home, Mr. Hotchkiss, when we picked up a young boy we thought was Johnny McGuire. It was a mistake, so the officers will be back shortly."

Ralph tried to make his voice sound sane. "We're being shot at. A bullet came through our front window just a few seconds ago!"

"Turn off the lights and keep down. "We'll go after the boy at once. You'll have protection within five minutes."

"I hope we last that long," Hotchkiss retorted. His nerves were quivering so badly he was unable to think what he was saying. Then something approaching sanity returned. "I'm sorry, I'm afraid I'm not myself."

"Understood, now get those lights off." Tibbs hung up.

"Dad, what's happening?" came from behind Hotchkiss. He turned quickly to find his son.

"Down on the floor, Billy, now!" he ordered, then he ran to the light switch and turned it off. Feeling the shielding comfort of the darkness, he returned to where he had left his family prone in the middle of the floor.

"That was Tibbs, the policeman," he said. "He told us to keep down and to turn off the lights. They'll be back any minute."

"I hope so," his wife answered him, a strange calmness in her voice.

Then it was quiet in the Hotchkiss household. Billy, knowing that he was the cause of it all, needed no cautioning to make him remain still. He tried to stay absolutely motionless and regulated his breathing as best he could.

Outside faint traffic noises could be heard; from almost a block away a city bus made familiar churning sounds as it pulled away from the curb. From inside the house the soft whirr of an electric clock could just be detected.

Then headlights came down the street and there was the sharper, clearer sound of vehicles pulling up and stopping.

"The police are back." Hotchkiss raised himself enough to peer out the window. He saw two official cars with red lights on and a third just arriving. A few moments later there was a knock at the door. "Mr. Hotchkiss, can you hear me?" a voice asked.

"Yes, clearly."

"Good. We're back and looking for the boy now. We have men all around your home, but stay where you are, with the lights off, until we can make a thorough check. We don't want to take any chances."

"Agreed." Nevertheless after a minute or two Hotchkiss sat up, satisfied that the danger was past, and looked out the window. Across the street, in the wooded area, he could see flashing lights and hear the voices of several men. Then compassion returned to him and he hoped that they would not hurt the boy when they found him. In the cool calmness of the darkened room he realized that they would not do that. He also began to understand how deeply his own son must have injured the youngster outside.

He also thought that the father had to be some kind of an idiot to keep a loaded revolver where a child could get at it.

Again there was a knock on the door, a quieter one this time. "This is Mr. Tibbs," Ralph heard. "You can turn on the lights now, Mr. Hotchkiss. And I'd like to come in if you please."

Stiffly and uncertain of himself, he got up, went to the light switch, and then opened the door. He found Tibbs there and also Barry Rothberg. As the policemen came in Estelle Hotchkiss got to her feet; her composure was badly shaken, but she made an effort nonetheless. "Will you have some coffee?"

"Thank you," Tibbs said. "We're a little shaken too."

That broke the ice. "I'm very sorry for the experience you've just been through," Virgil said to his host. "I told you what happened; we put two and two together and got the wrong four. If Chief Addis feels that it was our fault for pulling the protection away from your home too soon, and he very well may, then we'll pay for the window and the damage to your woodwork."

Hotchkiss shook his head. "Never mind that, we're insured. I only hope now that you find the boy and get the gun away from him before anything more happens."

"Amen," Tibbs agreed.

There was a strained silence for a short while, then Estelle Hotchkiss reappeared with a tray of empty coffee cups, cream, and sugar. "The kettle's on," she announced. "It will just be a couple of minutes." She set out the cups carefully in front of her husband and the two policemen.

Although he was at the moment a guest, Virgil's thoughts were very much elsewhere. He kept listening for any indication from the men outside that the boy had been found. If and when he was, then it was his intention to take him home himself and make sure that the child was not ill-treated. Having formed his estimate of Mike McGuire, he considered it a definite possibility that he might have to remain present until Johnny was at least safely in bed.

Estelle came in with the coffee and poured it out with hands which shook just a little. "Will they find him?" she asked.

"I believe so," Tibbs answered her easily. "He's only a small boy and he can't get too far on foot. It may take a little while because we don't want to frighten him any further if we can avoid it, and of course we have to recover the gun he has, or had, without any more accidents."

"What will you do to him?" Billy asked.

"I'm going to take him home myself," Virgil answered, "and help him if I can. He's not as old as you are, you know."

Billy hung his head. "Will you arrest him?"

"I don't think so. Part of the decision there rests with your father."

The telephone rang and Billy jumped to answer it. He listened for only a moment and then held out the instrument; Tibbs took it, spoke his name, and then actually seemed to turn pale. "I'll go there directly," he said and hung up.

He turned toward his hostess. "I'm very sorry," he apologized, "but I have to leave at once. Please excuse me." Within seconds he was out of the door and literally running for his car. Because of the time element it was hard for him to connect what had happened so recently at the Hotchkiss home with the report he had just been given, but he felt a definite tightening of his nerves.

He headed westward, driving as rapidly as he could without going into code three condition, toward a familiar destination. As he did so he tried to decide if it was possible that Johnny McGuire had somehow made his way without delay to another part of the city, or whether he now had two similar cases on his hands.

He pulled up and parked near to the emergency entrance of the Huntington Memorial Hospital. As he went inside he noted at once a gangling Negro youth who was waiting in the corridor. He knew that he wanted to talk to this young man, but his first concern was for the patient who had just been brought in. The receptionist nurse, who knew him, quickly shook her head. "You'll have to wait, Mr. Tibbs," she told him. "The boy is in critical condition; they've taken him into surgery. Even if he pulls through, I'm pretty sure you won't be able to see him tonight. At least I don't think so." As she finished speaking she inclined her head, very slightly, toward the teen-ager standing in the hallway.

"Thank you," he said. "If you get any further word, let me know immediately. Will you, please?"

"Of course — I've already asked them to keep me informed."

In a manner which seemed almost casual Tibbs turned away from the desk, walked down the corridor a short way, and then turned to speak to the obviously tense youth who seemed to be not quite sure where he was. "Did you bring in the boy who was shot?" he asked.

The young man looked slightly down at him from his six foot height and took his time before he answered. "Yeah, that's me."

"A friend of yours?" Tibbs asked.

Despite his obvious tension, the young Negro took a studied time before he answered. Then he said simply, "Yeah."

"It's a good thing you brought him immediately," Tibbs told him. "It's possible that you may have saved his life."

He was ignored.

This was not a new game, he had encountered it many times before. Pretending he had not noticed, he took his own time before he put his next question. Then he asked, "What happened?"

The Negro youth lifted his shoulders by way of reply and then let them settle back into position.

Once more Tibbs waited, then he reached into his pocket, pulled out a small leather case, opened it, and displayed his badge. He very seldom did that, if he had to offer credentials he preferred a simple calling card. In this instance the badge itself was the proper answer.

"Why didn't cha tell me?" the tall boy asked.

"I just did." There was no edge to the words, they came out only as a flat statement. "Who are you?"

The teen-ager shifted his weight. "Charlie Dempsey. They call me Sport."

"What happened, Sport?"

"Well, we was out drivin' in my car, doin' nothin' much, when we seen this kid. He looked like he was real lost so I stopped. I figured maybe he needed some help."

"Just like that."

Again the shoulders rose and fell in a slow movement. "I figured if we took the kid home, we might get a dollar or two for the trouble."

Tibbs nodded his head slowly as if that explanation had satisfied him. "Did you get out?"

"No, Beater, he got out. Nice and friendly-like he walked up to the kid. When they started talking then we all got out, I did and so did Jeff and Harry. Jus' got out, that's all. As soon as we got up near to the kid he called us a bunch o' niggers."

"I don't like that word," Tibbs said.

For the first time Dempsey looked at him with something like interest in his eyes.

"Well we didn't like it neither and we tol' him so. Just nice like. He was only a little kid."

"Was he wearing a jacket?"

"Yeah?"

"What color?"

"Red."

"New?"

"Naw, old. His arms was stickin' out the elbows."

"What about the gun?"

"Well, all we seen was this paper bag he had. Beater, he asked the kid what was in it and he said his lunch."

"You didn't believe that."

" 'Course not. Then all of a sudden the bag falls off, there the kid is standin' with the gun. First I thought it was a water pistol or somethin', then the kid he says it's real."

"Did you believe him?"

The Negro youth's voice rose slightly. "Mister, I wasn't takin' no chances on that. I started to edge around him so's I could grab him from the back. Jeff and Harry, they went for the sides. Beater, he stayed where he was in front. With the kid pointin' the gun at him he didn't dare go noplace."

Tibbs glanced down the hall toward the nurse receptionist, but she seemed occupied in working with a form on her desk.

"And then?"

Again the maddening shoulder shrug before the answer came. "The kid, he tried to jerk away, same time he fired the gun and hit Beater right in the guts. The damn little monkey shot him in cold blood."

71

"Go on."

"Well, Beater, he grabbed hisself and went down. Mister, I was too scared to know what I did. I let the kid go; I think he fired again, but I ain't sure, then he turned and run like hell. We didn't give no damn for him; we laid Beater out in the car and I brought him here."

"Where are the others?"

"They went home."

Tibbs produced his notebook. "Where do you live, Sport?" he asked. Dempsey gave him his address and those of his other two associates.

"Tell me about Beater, what sort of a fellow is he?"

This time there was no preliminary shoulder shrug, instead the boy seemed glad to answer the question. "Beater, he's got talent, he can do anythin'. Real sharp. He's a great cat on the skins, as good as they come, s'why we call him Beater. Good in a fight, clean like, good talker. He's got it all."

"Good friend of yours?"

"Best I got."

That sobered Tibbs, knowing what he did about the injured boy's condition. He flared with inner anger at the senselessness of it all. The loaded gun kept where a child had access to it; the idiotic mistake of grabbing a badly frightened boy from the rear when he was holding a gun and someone was standing directly in front of him.

Guns, dammit, guns! The right to keep and bear arms was given when a raw young country was part of a great, wild, largely unknown continent. In crowded modern cities a loaded gun was as lethal as a pit viper, a machine for killing and nothing else. Killing. First there was Kennedy and the bitter, terrible reality of a presidential assassination. Then Martin Luther King, as a Negro Tibbs could never forget that one. Because King had been more than just a prominent public figure who had been cut down; he had been the whole pride and hope of a long-suffering people, a man whose voice was listened to everywhere — and respected. The manhunt for his killer had been one of the most intensive in all history, but that did not bring King back, or his words, or give back to the Negro people their Nobel Prize winning peacemaker.

Then Robert Kennedy — three bullets from a small .22 had stopped his energy, his intensive drive, erased his victory over Eugene McCarthy, terminated in mid-flight his bid for the Presidency. One man, any man, could do it at any time.

It bit deeply into Tibbs's being because so many who had fallen had been Negroes, leaders who had offended the Southern white establishment. And among the dead lay the white mailman who had gone to the South to ask for fairness for his fellowmen and who had left his life there.

Because someone had a gun, a gun he could buy as easily as a stick of gum. Now Johnny McGuire was still in the city somewhere, still loose, still frightened, and still armed with a gun with several live bullets nested in its chambers.

For a few seconds Virgil had a hard time controlling himself. He saw before him the face of Mike McGuire, who ruthlessly forced other cars off the road when he was piqued, who in his ignorance considered himself to be a superior being, and who kept a gun to feed his vanity and cover his weaknesses.

In rage and frustration he clamped his teeth and cursed the day he had become a policeman. Then he would not have had to face things like this. But they would still be happening. whether he saw them with his own eyes or not. And until the last bullet was out of Johnny McGuire's gun, or until he was captured and the weapon was safely taken from him, who knew *what* could happen.

The nurse down the hall picked up her phone in answer to a short, subdued ring. She listened and then motioned to Virgil Tibbs who walked quickly down to where he could speak with her.

"I'm sorry, Mr. Tibbs, it's all over," she said. "They did everything possible, but it was no use. The boy died in surgery two or three minutes ago."

7

A sense of weariness and galling defeat hit Virgil
Tibbs; for the moment life to him was not worth the living.

Somewhere in the interior of the hospital a promising
boy he had never met lay dead, his life taken from him before
he had hardly begun to live. Somewhere in the city there
would be parents, anxious parents by now, to whom someone would have to carry a terrible message. Somewhere else
there was an irresponsible boy, armed and dangerous, who
in his desperation, might shoot again.

He would have to go back to the McGuires now and
break the news of what had happened. Then, somehow, he
would have to find and disarm their son. He understood
perfectly how the boy had been frightened, he knew that the
fatal shooting had been accidental, but that did not resolve

the problem. Because of his own dark skin, it might even compound it: if he came face-to-face with Johnny McGuire the boy would hardly now turn to him for help. It was more likely that he would think him a vengeful parent or older brother of the boy he had shot.

Tibbs went back up the corridor to where the lanky adolescent was still waiting. "I've just had a report," he said.

"Is he gone?" the boy asked.

Tibbs nodded. "They lost him in surgery, trying their utmost to save his life. So he didn't know, he was asleep."

There was a dead, thick silence.

"I'm gonna find that kid and kill him," Sport said. Not to Tibbs, but to the world around him, as far as it would reach.

"No. We'll find the boy. We'll get the gun and take him into custody."

"I'm gonna kill him," Dempsey repeated.

"You won't, you must not. For one thing, he isn't the only guilty person."

"Then who is?" the boy asked, burning Tibbs with his eyes.

"There's more than one person. His father, for keeping a gun where he could find it. Some Washington lobbyist who fought firearms control. Some legislators who went along with him because he was a good fellow."

"You gonna tell his family?" Sport asked. "I don' wanna have to do that."

Tibbs looked down at his hands to see if they would hold steady. He had had an exhausting day well before the first call on this job had come in, now he was physically and emotionally near to the end of his reserves. "I guess I'll have to," he said.

The sound of footsteps in the corridor made him look up; a young man in a clerical collar was approaching. "Mr. Tibbs, I'm Pastor Phillips," he said and shook hands briefly. "I understand a little of what has happened. Can I be of any help?"

Tibbs introduced Dempsey and supplied a condensed account of the evening's events.

"Has the family been notified?" the minister asked.

Tibbs shook his head. "I suspect that will be my job."

"Let me." He turned toward Dempsey. "Let's go together, since you know them. I may be able to offer spiritual comfort — poor people."

"Pastor, if you would care to do that, it would be a great help to me," Tibbs acknowledged. "I have another family to see."

The minister laid his arm across the shoulders of the awkward boy. "Shall we go?" he invited. With calm assurance he led him down the corridor and outside.

"Thank God for him — literally," Virgil said to himself and returned to the admittance desk where he could phone. He reported and was told in return that the watch over the Hotchkiss house would remain in effect on a twenty-four hour basis until Johnny McGuire had been captured. A stake-out was also set up at the McGuire home in the hope that the missing boy would come back on his own. Now, however, things were different and he would have to be taken into custody.

There was nothing new about the boy. One of Tibbs's fellow investigators came on the line briefly; he had made a quick check of the area where the shooting had taken place. Two families where lights had been on had admitted that they had heard "a noise" which might have been a shot or shots. Neither had reported it, one householder claimed he had thought it was a backfire from a hopped-up car, the other flatly admitted that whatever it had been, he hadn't wanted to get involved. The investigator had not bothered to explain that a properly equipped ambulance, if one had been called promptly, might have made the difference between survival or death; it would have been a waste of breath.

Notebook in hand, Virgil asked the admissions nurse for the proper name of the deceased, he had only heard him described as "Beater." The efficient, middle-aged woman consulted the work sheet before her. "Willie Orthcutt," she reported, and supplied the address. "That's all that I have now, Mr. Tibbs, there should be some more details later."

He drew in his breath and held it, then he let it out slowly while he thought. His mind at that moment was very active; unconsciously he passed a hand across his forehead as though to wipe away invisible perspiration.

"Mr. Tibbs, would you like a sedative?" the nurse offered. "Just something to quiet your nerves?"

"Thank you, but I wouldn't dare — at least not now. When I get home tonight, if I ever do, I'm going to mix myself a strong drink, listen to Ravel, and read the Book of Job."

"Why don't you do that right now."

"Impossible, you know that. Do me a favor, phone headquarters and give them what facts you have about the shooting victim. I have to follow up on the boy with the gun."

"Take care of yourself," the nurse admonished as he turned to leave.

Fifteen minutes later Tibbs was back in the kitchen of the McGuire apartment. "You oughtn't to come here so much," Mike told him. "We're looking for our boy to come home, but he won't if you're hanging around all the time."

Tibbs was in no mood to be unduly polite. "It doesn't matter now," he said, and let it hang there.

Maggie had the first inkling, she looked up at him from where she sat, her eyes widening in renewed fright. "Has he done something?" she asked, forcing the words out from between her lips.

Virgil nodded. "I'm very sorry, Mrs. McGuire, desperately sorry, but I'm afraid that he has. Another boy, about fourteen years of age."

Mike McGuire was suddenly sobered, his wounded pride was put aside. "Did he — hurt him?" he asked.

For Maggie's sake Tibbs forced down the impulse to give it to him right between the eyes. "Something like an hour ago Johnny fired a shot into the Hotchkiss home, at least we are assuming it was your son. Fortunately no one was hurt."

"Then who . . . ?" Mike asked.

"Somehow, I'm not sure how, Johnny apparently made his way to the west side of the city. There four boys out in a car stopped him, again I can't say for certain that it was your boy, and a scuffle followed."

"What were they trying to do to him?" Mike asked in quick suspicion.

"I don't know for sure, Mr. McGuire, one of them told me they thought he was lost and hoped they could earn a dollar or two taking him home. I don't entirely believe that, but there is no evidence so far that they had any criminal intent. Whatever the circumstances, Johnny apparently became frightened and fired the gun. I don't believe that he did it on purpose."

"And . . . ?" Maggie asked.

"One of the boys was hit, in the abdomen, I understand. I'm very, very sorry, Mrs. McGuire, to have . . ."

"Is the boy all right?" she interrupted him, her voice rising.

He shook his head. "He died in the hospital a few minutes ago."

She buried her face in her folded arms. Tibbs looked

at McGuire whose color was now ashen. "If by any chance you see your son before I do, don't under any circumstances tell him about the death. If he still has the gun . . ."

"I'll take it away from him," he promised. "You can have the damned thing, I don't want it any more."

"Exactly what kind of a gun is it?" Tibbs asked. "I know you said that it is a Colt .38, but that covers several models. Can you be more specific?" The question helped just a little to restore some emotional balance in the small room.

"It's called a Chief's Special," Mike answered. "You know about it?"

"Yes, I do. I think you'd like to be alone now; you don't need to expect me back any more this evening."

"What if you find Johnny?"

Virgil Tibbs considered that for a moment. "In view of what's happened, we'll have to hold him — at least temporarily. But it might be the best thing for him, and for his mother, if we brought him here for a little while first."

Mike rubbed his jaw with the flat of his hand. "That's decent of you," he said, and for the moment paid his guest the supreme compliment of overlooking his heritage.

One more weary time Tibbs drove back to headquarters and made his report. Then, his duty done for the time being, he headed for home. In his own car he drove to his apartment, turned on the lights, and gratefully kicked off his shoes. Despite the fact he had not eaten, the idea of food did not attract him. Instead he mixed himself a drink, sat down stiffly on one end of his davenport, and nourished his spirit by studying a magnificent painting which hung on the opposite wall. It was an outdoors scene which proclaimed itself to be California; dominating the picture as its central subject was a lovely young woman. She had deep blue, widely separated eyes, golden blond hair brilliant in the strong light. She looked out of the canvas, directly at Virgil, proud and unconcerned by her nudity. Her perfectly formed breasts were not on display, they were simply part of her which added to the all-over perfection of her body.

To Virgil Tibbs the picture meant far more than the considerable cash value it represented. An original by William Holt-Rymers was entirely beyond his means, but this one was not only a gift from the artist, it had also been done particularly for him without his knowledge and the subject had sat for it as her contribution.

Presently the alcohol took the sharp edge off his fatigue; he reminded himself that he had had nothing to eat since noon. He got to his feet and raised his glass a few inches toward the picture.

"Thank you, Linda," he said half aloud. The ritual completed he changed into a comfortable yukata, put a new recording of *Miroirs* on his stereo system, and opened his refrigerator door.

When he awoke in the morning the fact that his phone had not rung told him that Johnny McGuire had not been located. It also implied that the gun he carried had been silent. By eight-thirty he was in his office, facing a pile of work which was always waiting on his desk. Bob Nakamura, his unofficial partner and office mate, sat a few feet away embroiled in his own case file. The weather outside was fine, the only redeeming feature of what otherwise promised to be a grim and possibly tragic day.

There was nothing new whatever concerning Johnny McGuire.

As soon as he had taken care of some urgent details left over from another case, Tibbs went to see Captain Lindholm, the chief of the detective bureau. After exchanging a brief greeting, he plunged directly into the thought which was in his mind. "I lost a bet last night," he admitted. "I was confident, at first, that the McGuire boy would go home. He didn't — you know what happened."

The captain nodded. "He could have been too frightened or else got lost, pure and simple."

Tibbs nodded. "I can buy it either way, sir, although I like the second a little better. Another thought — you know where the shooting took place. It's only about five blocks from the Arroyo Seco. If the boy was lost, or too scared to go home, he might have hidden somewhere in the park. That is, if he knew it was there."

Lindholm smiled. "I've had two men in plain clothes down there for the past hour. I'd like to send more, but we had two armed robberies after you went home last night."

"What do you want me to do?"

"Stick on the McGuire thing by all means. Let me know if you get into a corner or need more help."

"Thank you," Virgil said, and left.

Twenty minutes later Tibbs was back at the Huntington Memorial Hospital. The surgical team which had worked to save the life of Willie Orthcutt would have left a report. Because of something he had noticed the previous night, he was most anxious to see it.

Although no postmortem had as yet been performed, the preliminary findings were quite clear. The fatal bullet had entered the abdomen on a straight line, indicating that it had been fired from a point approximately three feet above the ground. Had prompt medical attention been available on the scene before the victim had been moved, he might have been saved, but this was highly problematical.

There was also a second wound, this one in the upper forearm. Assuming that the two shots had been fired from the same point, then rough triangulation, according to the surgeon's estimate, gave the distance as between ten and fifteen feet. The bullet in the abdomen had entered just below the normal position of the belt buckle and had traveled in an almost exactly horizontal line; the one in the forearm had entered through the biceps muscle and had struck the bone. The triangulation presumed that both shots had been fired at almost the same time, otherwise a standing posture on the part of the victim could no longer be assumed.

84

The rest of the medical report was technical, but ended with the unqualified statement that death had been caused by the abdominal bullet which had passed entirely through the body. The fact that the spine had not been struck was immaterial in view of the fact that death had taken place. Tibbs absorbed the information with a sense of satisfaction; it was a thoroughly professional job of putting facts on paper. This saved much time and provided a piece of reliable evidence for the use of the Juvenile Court.

The hospital visit concluded, Tibbs drove to the address he had been given for the boy called Jeff. When he arrived, he found a modest home where the whole family was gathered, clearly in anticipation of an official visit. In the course of his work his racial heritage had often been a handicap to him. This time it might make things somewhat easier.

The parents of the boy greeted him as well as could be expected; they were obviously respectable, decent people who were seriously upset and fearful of the fact that their son was involved in a case of manslaughter. Jeff himself was there together with three sisters of varying ages who seemed content to remain still and unnoticed.

"All I can say, Mr. Tibbs," Jeff's mother began, "is that I'm thankful to God that the white boy didn't shoot our son. It's Jesus' grace that he didn't." She was a big woman, well over two hundred pounds, but when she gathered her boy to her, she became only a relatively helpless mother striving to protect what was nearest and dearest to her.

85

Following the usual preliminaries Virgil turned his attention to Jeff. "What's your full name, son?" he asked gently.

"Jeffrey William Howell."

"All right, Jeffrey, as far as I know now you aren't personally in any trouble and you don't need to worry."

"Thank God," his father said in an unexpectedly rich bass. He was a thin man whose face and hands both testified to many years of physical labor. He stood quietly in the corner of the humble room.

Virgil was glad at that moment that he was a Negro, that he could establish empathy with these people who had been caught in the crossfire of a serious police case. At least to them the law did not have an exclusively white face.

The boy's mother picked up the reins. "Mr. Tibbs, I've been worried sick about his running around in that hopped-up car. I know they're his friends, but it isn't right. It could have been him; it could have been our boy." She hastily wiped her eyes.

"In your opinion, why does he go with that particular crowd?" Tibbs asked.

The fleshy woman recovered enough to answer. "Because of the boy they call Sport. He's older; he owns the car. He's the big man and they all want to run with him. And then there's Luella."

"Luella?"

"Yes. As far as I know she's a nice enough girl, not

86

wild or anything like that, but the boys all like her maybe a little too much."

"Oh, ma," Jeffrey said.

"Well you know that it's true enough, you told me so yourself." She returned her attention to her visitor. "Let's just say that Luella's popular. She's sort of Sport's girl, but she gets along with all the boys in the crowd, sometimes she goes out with them."

"That sounds very reasonable," Tibbs commented.

"I guess that it is — what I meant is that Jeffrey, like all the other boys I guess, likes her and that's one reason he goes with Sport and the others."

"Thank you. Now, Jeffrey, tell me all about it, just as it happened."

In the presence of his parents and of the law the boy was in a chastened mood. He told his version without ornamentation, hesitating from time to time as he realized the gravity of the circumstances in which he had been involved.

He had little that was new to offer; his story closely paralleled the one given to Tibbs by Charles Dempsey. In a few minor details he differed; Tibbs was well aware that the mark of a truthful witness is agreement on major points mixed with disagreement on smaller ones. Few people have perfect memories, especially concerning occasions when they were under unusual stress.

In one particular area Tibbs was explicit in his questioning — the moment when the first shot had been fired. It was most important to determine if Johnny McGuire had pulled the trigger of his own volition or if he had done so involuntarily as a result of having been unexpectedly grabbed from behind.

Jeffrey did his best to answer. "Well, Beater, he was standin' still like, he wasn't goin' for the kid at all. Then Sport, he grabbed him real quick. The white kid, he twisted like, fightin' to get away. That's when it happened."

"Exactly what happened then?"

"Beater, I mean Willie, he grabbed himself in the guts, I knew right then he'd been hit."

"Did he say anything?"

"Not then. After maybe a second or two he made a noise, like he was hurt."

"Now, Jeffrey, I want you to think carefully, because this is *very* important. Exactly what did the white boy do after he fired the gun and hit Willie in the abdomen?"

Jeffrey shook his head. "I don't know," he admitted. "I was awful scared. I'd been right by Willie, I only just got away in time."

"Did anything else happen that you noticed, anything at all?"

The boy collected himself. "I don't remember exactly. Sport, he yelled to watch out and let go of the kid, or the kid got away, I ain't sure. I think the white kid he shot again, but like I said, I ain't sure — it was all so fast. Anyhow, Willie he fell down and the white kid, he run like hell. I didn't want to chase him."

"I can understand that," Virgil agreed.

"Then Sport, he said we'd have to take Willie to the hospital right away. He picked him up."

"Alone?"

"Yeah, Sport, he's strong. Willie, he was cryin' when Sport put him in the back o' the car. Then he told us to beat it before any cops come and he drove off."

"Why did you call him 'Beater'?"

" 'Cause he was a real good drum man. He had a beat, he had."

"Then what did you do?"

"I came home."

"Did you tell your family what had happened?"

The boy hung his head. "No. I figured Willie would be maybe all right and I didn't want to get into no trouble."

With that interview behind him Tibbs drove to the home of the boy called Harry, the fourth member of the group which had accosted Johnny McGuire. He was not there; his mother reported that he was working in a car wash a few blocks away. With the cooperation of the wash rack manager he spent a half hour with the last of the witnesses and found him slightly more articulate than Jeffrey had been. Once again he heard substantially the same story, the only significant addition came when Harry timed the second shot as having followed almost at once. He was also definite that Johnny had been still struggling with his captor at the time.

After close questioning designed to get behind the

ingrained hostility which the boy had allowed to build up massively in his mind, Tibbs determined that Harry was grudgingly of the opinion that both of the shots had been accidental. He was relieved that he had been able to develop this information. While Harry's opinion would not be admissible in court, it being a conclusion of the witness, a good defense attorney would be able to bring it out.

Grimly satisfied that he had learned all that he could from Harry at the moment, Tibbs got back into his car. He had to go now and find Johnny McGuire. He had to calm him down, get his gun away from him, and bring him safely into the police station. He also had to do something about the McGuires, by now Johnny's mother would be frantic.

Hopefully he had to do all this before any militants could arrive on the scene. If they and their followers were to pour in and start their own search for the McGuire boy, disaster and tragedy would hang in the balance. Johnny McGuire had already fired his gun three times and was probably in a near crazed state of mind. He would no longer be in the heat of rage, but he was now outside the law and old enough to grasp that fact. To avoid capture he might in desperation fire again, and there were still bullets in his gun.

8

Johnny McGuire awoke early in the morning. As soon as the full light of day began to penetrate the thicket in which he had taken refuge he opened his eyes, remembered, and then lay still.

For a few moments he felt terribly alone and had an almost overwhelming urge to rush to the wonderful shelter of his mother. Then an even more powerful voice told him that to do that might mean disaster.

He relived again the nightmare that had happened to him on that dark, silent street. Once more he saw the four older boys approaching him, felt the weight of their size, and the pressure of their number. He had never intended to fire the gun, he had not done it on purpose, but it still had been his hand that had pulled the trigger.

Like a hypnotic dream in which every normal motion is slowed to an agonizing pace that will not be hurried, he felt again the unexpected hands gripping his arms from behind. He felt himself trying to lunge forward, but his movements were torturously slowed. Then his hands tightened into fists in order to fight back, that involuntary motion had pulled the trigger.

He heard again the terrible blast of sound and felt once more the mighty kick of the gun in his hand. He saw once more the boy standing before him, then watched as he folded his arms across his abdomen and began to sink to the ground.

He lived again the paralyzing terror of that moment: the shocked seconds of confusion; the sight of the boy he had shot crumbling to the ground and he was aware of nothing else until he knew that he was running away. It seemed as though he were running through water up to his waist; he was not wet, but some unseen force was holding him back so that he could not move except very, very slowly. It was a battle each time he lifted a knee high enough to run. . . .

Abruptly he came back to the present as he realized that he could not remain where he was much longer undiscovered. People were not up yet, but they would be soon and he would have to make good his escape. He wanted desperately to go home, and he thought about it carefully. He had seen the police cars in front of Billy Hotchkiss's house and he knew that the goddamn cops were after him. They would also know who had shot the black boy in the street. Of course it was not as serious as it would have been if he had been white, but they would be mad at him just the same. They might even arrest him for it.

Just like the shows on TV, they would wait for him at his home. That meant he could not go there now, he would have to wait until evening and after they had quit for the day. Conscience prodded him with the bitter fact that his mother would be terribly worried, he had never stayed away from home overnight before. He drew in a quick sob of breath when he thought of her, he wanted her so much! Bitterly he forced himself to realize that he couldn't see her for several more hours, it was part of the price he had to pay for shooting into Billy Hotchkiss's home.

He had to have somewhere to go, somewhere to stay that the goddamn cops couldn't find him. They would know him right away by his jacket because everyone did, they kidded him about it at school. It was warm on him now, but because it was his only jacket, and the only one he could remember ever having had, he loved it. Then he reasoned it out. Carefully he took it off, folded it inside out so that the red color would not show, and tucked it into the base of the thickest bush. Tomorrow, he resolved, he would come and get it back.

He wondered if he should leave the gun too. If he did, he would be free of it at last and the danger it would represent if he were caught. Then he remembered the black faces he had seen only dimly in the dark, one of them was sick now, but the other three would be out for his blood. If one of them found him, and he didn't have his gun, he might be killed.

As best he could he considered the matter, weighing one danger against the other. He could not decide until he remembered the evening when he had sat beside his strong and wise father and had first been shown the gun and had it explained to him. "A gun is a good thing," his father had said. "Because sometime you might have to protect yourself or your ma. Maybe sometime two or three of 'em will come at you and you won't have a chance. Then the gun makes you the boss; when they see a gun they stop real quick. When you've got a gun, nobody's gonna give you no trouble."

The decision to keep the gun made for him, he wondered now where he could go. He had all day to spend, but if he just walked the streets it would be too dangerous. He had no relatives he could go to, no friend he could trust. Then, out of the clear blue, a sudden and wonderful idea rushed upon him, an idea charged with electric possibilities. He could go to the baseball game!

He could go and see the Angels themselves, the real players, the big league stars in action. It almost took his breath away, but it was possible. He had more than fifteen dollars in his pockets and it was his own money. He had no idea where Anaheim was, but thousands of people went there every day to the great stadium.

94

Then, as though his own dedicated guardian angel had spoken to him, he remembered that he did have a friend after all, a great and powerful friend! With shaking fingers he pulled out his little plastic wallet and extracted a worn piece of paper. He had carried it so much, and had read it so many times, it barely held together at the folds. With great care he opened it and read once more the words he could easily have repeated from memory:

Dear Johnny:

Thank you for your nice letter. I'm glad you want to become a catcher for the Angels, the best thing to do is to drink your milk and practice every day that you can.

I'm very flattered that you want to meet me so much. The next time that you are at the ball park, bring this letter to the clubhouse door and show it to the guard. He will let me know and I'll be glad to come out and shake hands with you.

Your friend,
Tom Satriano

Now he knew what to do. Somehow, some way, he must get to Anaheim. With the precious letter he would get to meet Tom Satriano himself. He might have all of his equipment on, his shin guards, the big pad across his chest, and the mask behind which he watched every motion of the game. And he would see Tom Satriano play! He would see him crouching behind the plate, signaling the pitcher what to

95

throw, running back to catch foul balls, and cutting down base stealers with the whiplike power of his arm.

Another wonderful thought tumbled into his mind: when he met Tom Satriano he could tell him what had happened and Tom would help him and tell him what to do. He would know, because he was the catcher and ran the whole baseball team on the field. Tom Satriano was a big leaguer, a very important man, so important that he probably knew Gene Autry himself.

Now time was beginning to press him, if anyone saw him leaving his hiding place, it could be the end of everything right there. He would have to go now, while he still had a chance. He listened, then peeked through and looked, but he saw or heard nothing which threatened danger. Pushing the shoe box ahead of him he crawled from underneath the bushes, brushed himself off, and looked for a path that would take him back to the streets of Pasadena.

Ten minutes later the attendant at an all-night filling station was mildly surprised to see a small boy with a shoe box under his arm come trudging up the driveway. "You're up awful early, aren't you?" he asked, amused at the boy's slightly bedraggled appearance.

Johnny knew one reason why a boy might be up at that hour and he was quick to use it. "I've got a paper route," he explained. "May I use the bathroom?"

"Sure, go ahead."

In the momentary shelter of the rest room Johnny

relieved himself and then washed carefully. When he picked up his shoe box again, the gun inside slid over and made a noise. Although the door could open and someone could come in at any moment, Johnny knew that something would have to be done. From the waste container he retrieved a number of crumpled paper towels. With these he padded the inside of the box and then laid his gun on top. He replaced the lid and shook the box experimentally; there was no heavy *clunk* to give him away.

Satisfied with his work, he returned to the service area and asked, "Can you tell me which way is Anaheim?" Then, quickly, he added, "My dad is going to take me there today."

"Anaheim?" the attendant said. "I bet I know where you're going. You're going to Disneyland, aren't you."

Johnny nodded. "Yes, but we aren't sure how to get there."

The man stepped inside the office and returned with a map. "Here, let me show you." He spread it out across his knee. "Here's Anaheim, down off the Santa Ana Freeway. Do you live near here?"

"Yes, we do."

"Good, then the best way will be for your father to take the Pasadena Freeway to the interchange and then go through the slot until the Santa Ana branches off to the right. Can you remember all that?"

Johnny took the map. "I can remember, but sometimes our car doesn't run so good. Can we take the bus?"

"Yes, if you want to. Catch a number fifty-eight on Fair Oaks Avenue into Los Angeles. You can change there for a bus direct to Disneyland; it'll drop you off right at the main gate."

"Is that close to where the Angels play?"

The attendant nodded. "Sure, maybe a mile."

"Thanks a lot, mister."

"You're welcome, son."

Johnny's spirits rose rapidly as he turned back in the direction from which he had come. He knew now where Anaheim was and how to get there. He also had learned that every other human hand was not against him, he had talked with the man at the filling station and had had no trouble at all. His confidence grew despite the realization that his mother would be wondering where he was and that his father, if he found out, would be awful mad about his taking the gun.

In the bright new daylight the thing that had happened the night before seemed to be far away. The darkness and the fears that it had harbored were gone; the streets did not look the same and traffic was beginning to flow in a normal manner. For a slim moment he considered the possibility of trying to go home, then a host of considerations swept the thought away. The cops might be there, but what was much more important, he would lose his one chance to go to the ball game. In his whole life he might never have another.

When he reached Orange Grove Avenue no bus was in sight. With his shoe box still tucked carefully under his arm he stood at the bus stop for a minute or two, then decided it would be better if he could keep moving. He was too close to the place where he had fired the gun the night before; there was too great a risk that someone might spot him standing there.

Checking again that no bus was visible for several blocks, he began to walk southward in the general direction of Los Angeles. That helped him to feel much better, he was already on his way to Anaheim and every step that he took put the nightmare of the previous evening farther behind him. A few other people were beginning to appear now, in a little while he would no longer look so alone.

When he reached the next corner he walked to the curb and again looked up the street behind him for any sign of an approaching bus. At his feet there was a loose pile of throwaway newspapers, put there for some deliveryman to pick up.

Again there was no sign of a bus, but coming down the street less than a block away a police car was approaching, cruising slowly close to the curb. On the instant Johnny was flooded with a new and fearful sense of disaster, his confidence vanished and fear gripped him. He knew with frightening immediacy that he was still a hunted creature, but it was too late to run and hide.

Swiftly he bent over and picked up as many of the papers as he could with one hand. He threw them over his arm to conceal the shoe box, then squatted down and put another bunch on top. As he finished, the police car pulled up beside him and stopped.

There were two uniformed men in it; the one closest to him leaned out the window and said, "Morning, son, how are you feeling?"

"Fine."

"What's your name?"

"Mike."

"How long have you been delivering papers, Mike?"

"About two months."

"Have you seen another boy around here this morning, one with a worn-out red jacket?"

Johnny shook his head. "I just got here," he replied.

"OK, thanks a lot." The policeman waved a hand as the car moved away and continued down the street.

For the next ten minutes Johnny played his role as a newsboy, fearful only that the rightful holder of the job would arrive and challenge him. He walked rapidly down Orange Grove Avenue tossing a paper on the sidewalk or lawn before each house. As he did so he kept a careful watch back down the street for any sign of a bus that would rescue him from his precarious situation. He had almost run out of papers when he saw at last the square, flat face of the big vehicle two and a half blocks away. Breaking into a run, he dropped his remaining papers and reached the bus stop just in time to signal it to stop.

Having ridden a bus once before on his own, he

climbed up into the vehicle with assurance and offered the driver fifty cents.

"Los Angeles?" the man asked.

Johnny nodded and received a penny in change. He walked back and sat down full of a wonderful sense of escape. He had never enjoyed a bus ride so much; he was unhappy only when it stopped for other passengers and delayed his progress. He wished also that he could talk to his mother and tell her that he was all right. If she had been with him, then he would have felt infinitely better.

Maggie McGuire sat before her kitchen table, staring unseeing through the wall that faced her. She was alone. Mike had gone to work. He had wanted to stay home and wait for news of his son, but with the expensive citation hanging over his head he had reluctantly decided that he could not afford even a momentary loss of income. Maggie had promised to call him the moment there was any word.

The considerations of money and the hard realities of day-to-day living washed over her like breakers running up a sandy beach and then retreating back into the anonymous vastness from which they had come. Her baby was gone, and that single fact dominated her. She understood that he had killed another boy and that he would have to go to prison, but if she could only hold him for just one long, all-engulfing minute in her arms, then, she felt, she would be able to face up to almost anything.

He had been with her here less than twenty-four hours ago, and she had given him little or no attention. If she had just taken the time to look at him she might have seen the bulge of the fatal gun in his pocket or stuck in his clothing, but she hadn't bothered. Now, in the bitterness of her loss, she told herself that she was an unfit mother who had not taken proper care of the precious life entrusted to her. She put her head down and cried a little more. It was then that the phone rang.

Anxiously, fearfully, she picked it up.

"Mrs. McGuire?"

"Yes, yes!"

A worn-out, clacky voice began to recite a sales pitch about carpet and upholstery cleaning. The crews would be in the neighborhood and a free estimate . . .

"No!" she cried, and hung up the accursed instrument. Helplessly she beat her hands against the top of the table.

The phone rang again. "Yes?" she snapped.

A thin, small voice said, "Hello, Mommy."

She grasped the phone as though she could make the voice at the other end come closer. "Johnny?" she asked.

"I just wanted to tell you that I'm all right," her son said.

Her voice went dry and she could barely speak. "Where are you?" she asked.

"Right here in the phone booth, Mommy." A slight whimpering sound came over the wire. "Mommy, my radio's broken."

"I know, Johnny, that's all right. Don't worry, you'll get a new one."

"Is Daddy mad?"

"No, Daddy isn't mad. He knows that you didn't break it." A sense of reality began to come back to her and she tried to think. "Tell me where you are, dear, and I'll come." She knew when she spoke those words that she had no means of transportation, but she would even have called a taxi — anything — to reach him.

"Mommy, I think I'm in trouble." The voice was a little softer, a thread of guilt running through the words.

"Johnny, I don't care! Tell me where you are, Mommy wants you!"

"Mommy, I took Daddy's gun and I shot a nigger boy with it."

Maggie could stand no more, raw emotion shattered the little composure she had and caution deserted her.

"Johnny, I don't care if you *did* kill that boy, come home — Daddy will take care of you!"

There was a fearful silence.

"Mommy," came a very small voice, "did you say I *killed* him?"

"Johnny . . ." she began when another voice cut into the line. "Your three minutes are up. Please signal when you are finished."

After that she heard nothing for three or four seconds, then the mechanical sound of the handset on the other end being replaced. The connection was broken.

She wiped her eyes with the backs of her trembling hands, picked up the card which was next to the telephone and dialed.

When she had an answer she said, "Mr. Tibbs, please," and waited.

9

As he drove back toward his office, Virgil Tibbs realized that he would have to snap out of it. It did no good to tell himself that he did not know which way to turn next, it was his job to do the turning.

By the time he had parked and climbed one flight to the second floor he had managed to gather the right amount of resolve. He said hello to Bob Nakamura, glanced once at the accumulated pile of work which awaited him, and then sat down as a man should who is equal to the challenges before him. But before he could begin on anything, Bob had news for him.

"The cat's loose on your kid with the gun," he said. "It's on all the newscasts. You've had several frantic telephone calls, the usual sort. Someone from the National Rifle Association wants you to call him back. I could use your help on this double header we had last night, apparently the same gang pulled both jobs, but the captain says you can't be spared until the youngster has been picked up and disarmed. Any light?"

Tibbs shook his head. As Bob watched he pulled open a drawer and took out his service revolver. Very carefully he removed the six bullets that it contained. Then he checked the barrel, carefully reinspected the cylinder, and absolutely verified that the weapon was empty. "I want you to help me with something," he said in a voice that was collected and businesslike. "Come here, will you?"

Bob got to his feet and took the gun when it was offered to him.

"Check that it's empty."

Nakamura broke the Colt .38 open and gave it a careful scrutiny. "OK."

"All right, now turn your back on me. Imagine that you're holding a bead on someone about twelve or fifteen feet in front of you."

"Do I aim for his head or do I know what I'm doing?"

"Aim for the abdomen, but assume, if you can, that you have no real intention of shooting. You're not a marksman, you're a small boy who knows very little about handling a gun."

The Nisei detective turned so that he was facing the window and then pointed the gun steadily at an invisible target. Virgil let him stand there for a good half minute, until he knew that his partner's reflexes would be automatically slowed down. Then, without warning, he threw his arms around him from behind, catching him just above the elbows. Bob jerked back.

"Now," Tibbs asked, "under those circumstances could you have pulled the trigger accidentally?"

"Definitely, in fact it's possible that I did, I had my finger inside the guard."

"Next I want to try something else. As you were."

Obediently Bob resumed his pose, holding the gun horizontally in front of him as he imagined a child might do. Once more Virgil quickly grabbed his arms, held him for a few seconds, and then attempted to fit his right hand over the gun, his fingers on top of Nakamura's. Immediately his partner drew away and, turning to his left, aimed the gun squarely at Tibbs. "Is that what you wanted me to do?" he asked.

"Exactly. Now the question is just this: if for any reason I had wanted to, could I have forced you to fire the gun a second time? And if so, could I have guided your aim?"

Bob thought for a moment. "Possibly," he said with considerable hesitation. "But it would have to be a very long shot. The moment you let go with your right hand to grab the gun it was easy for me to twist away from you. Even assuming that I'm an untrained small boy."

"Then I'm satisfied on that point. I wasn't before."

Tibbs took the gun back, reloaded it, and replaced it in his desk drawer.

"Care to tell me what it's all about?" Nakamura asked.

"There isn't really anything to tell. I noticed something last night that set me thinking. It was pretty uncertain, but I wanted to check it out anyway."

His partner was ahead of him. "You were impersonating someone right now; a look at his record might be interesting."

Virgil nodded. "I'm planning to check it. You see, the gun was fired twice last night, during the scuffle I mean, when an older boy tried to grab Johnny McGuire. I saw a possibility that the bigger boy might have had something to do with that second shot."

"Did he ever have possession of the gun?"

"No."

"Then after the experiment we just tried, Virg, I can't see it. I'm sure you'd never get a conviction in court, even if you could show murderous hostility."

Tibbs did not reply, too many other ideas were piling up in his mind. He tried to deal with the matter of Johnny McGuire first, and against his better judgment decided to hope for the best. A small boy, even with sixteen dollars in his pocket, could not keep going on his own for too long. Probably he would have discarded his gun as too conspicuous, too heavy, or too dangerous to carry any longer. In that case after he was picked up, the job of recovering the weapon should be simple. That would be the easy way.

At any moment, he fervently hoped, the phone would ring with the news that Johnny had been seen somewhere or had managed to find his way home. Every patrol car, every policeman on duty, even the law enforcement personnel of all the nearby communities were now on the lookout for him. He rationalized that it would be the soundest procedure to sit tight and wait for a break.

Then he knew that he couldn't do that. The problem of Johnny McGuire, grave as it already was, had been intensified by the shadow of the militant black power advocates. These hardened professional agitators and their followers could descend on Pasadena and whip up a first-class riot in short order, despite the fact that police riot-handling tactics had improved considerably since the days of the terror in Watts.

He picked up the phone, but before he could place his call he was told that he had visitors in the lobby. Three minutes later Charles Dempsey and a young Negro girl were shown into his office. The boy acknowledged an introduction to Nakamura and then presented the young lady. "This is Luella," he said. "She wanted to come along."

Virgil placed chairs for them and invited them to sit down. The girl did so, but Dempsey preferred to remain on his feet. "I wanna find out what's happenin'," he began abruptly. "Because, man, you got trouble. Big trouble."

"I'm in the trouble business," Tibbs answered. "What do you want to tell me?"

"Well, right off Willie was a mighty popular boy, he'd

got a lot of friends. An' a lot of the guys are already lookin' for the white boy that shot him."

Tibbs turned to the girl. "Do you agree with that?" he asked.

Luella took a few moments to consider her answer. She was about fifteen and he noted that she was undeniably ripe for her age. Her features were somewhat on the aquiline side, her waist slender, her breasts conspicuously high and full. Her voice, when she spoke, gave evidence of some training. "Willie was a real comer, Mr. Tibbs. He was a smart boy, mighty good-looking, and he had a lot of real talent. He was going places."

"Damn right," Sport added. "An' I wanna tell ya that if any o' our guys get hold of that white boy with the gun, somethin's gonna happen."

"What do you think I should do?" Virgil asked.

Dempsey responded at once to the flattery; he leaned forward against the desk to emphasize his words. "Well, if you can put out that you got this kid in the can, and no smart lawyer's gonna get him right out again, it might make people feel a lot better. See he didn't shoot no ordinary kid — he shot a black boy. You know how things are."

"I know."

"Well maybe you don' know that right now they're gettin' a meetin' organized down in Brookside Park. And if it gets swingin', it ain't gonna be no picnic, you can bet on that."

Tibbs's face tightened for just a moment. "I want to make something clear to you," he said. "The person who shot your friend is still a little boy. That doesn't excuse or undo what he did, but a child of nine isn't wholly responsible for his actions."

The girl nodded, but Sport looked at him through narrowed eyes. "You sound like you're for this white kid. Are you with us or ain't ya?"

A pencil snapped between Virgil's fingers. "That has nothing to do with it, and you're old enough to know it. If you must look at it that way, then color me blue—I'm a policeman."

"Well I thought . . ." the youngster began, and then stopped.

"You mean that you're going to let the white boy go?" the girl asked. Her voice rose at the end of the sentence.

"No, of course not," Tibbs answered. "Nobody shoots anybody around here and gets away with it—or if he does it's because we did our very best and failed. But a murder case is never closed until it's resolved. And for that matter . . ." A shadow seemed to pass across his dark features. Whatever he was going to say remained unspoken, instead he added quietly, "You should know better than to ask that of me— or any other police officer."

"Look," Sport said, "I'm the big man around where I live, you just ask anybody. You get that kid an' I can make you look good—the cops, I mean. You remember 'bout

Watts? Well, a cop, he started that. I don't want nobody more to get hurt, so I can help you maybe, huh?"

"Fine," Tibbs answered. "That's a deal. Suppose you begin by passing the word that if anybody locates the boy, don't try to take him, call me. I'll see that you get all the credit, but your people are too valuable to get shot, OK?"

Dempsey revealed a wide toothy grin. "Leave it ta me," he promised.

As soon as he was well out of the office Bob Nakamura shook his head. "Virg, that line about his people being too valuable to get shot was a classic."

"It's perfectly true," Tibbs said.

"Of course it is, it's just the way that you put it. It implied, of course, that we're expendable and he ate it up. I don't think he's quite as stupid as he pretends to be."

"Of course not." Tibbs picked up his phone once more, called records and asked for a check on Charles Dempsey, about eighteen, Negro, and a self-proclaimed leader in the youth group. As soon as he had that working he called the MTA bus information number and inquired about the early evening schedule on the line which ran close to Billy Hotchkiss's home. After a few seconds delay he got exactly what he had suspected — confirmation that a bus had gone past at almost the same time that the shot had been fired. After that there had not been another for a full hour.

He silently cursed the luck that had given Johnny McGuire that convenient ride; if the shot he had fired into the Hotchkiss house had been delayed for only two or three minutes then the search for the boy would almost certainly have been successful and a tragic death would have been avoided. The more than ten years he had spent in police work had taught him, through frustrating experience, how often perverse breaks can go against the members of the force; for every good one that came along at least three others seemed always to go the wrong way.

The phone rang. It was records reporting that Charles Dempsey had had a total of six traffic moving violations, had been uncooperative twice when cited, and had been arrested fourteen months previously on suspicion of armed robbery. When faced with this last charge he had provided an alibi which had checked out. He had given enough information to establish his own innocence, but had refused to volunteer anything more.

Tibbs evaluated this. Being uncooperative while being cited was all too common — some of the most prominent citizens of Pasadena had that noted in their records. Nobody likes traffic tickets. Since the alibi had been proved, the armed robbery charge was out. It boiled down to a somewhat above average number of traffic tickets, two of which had made him mad. For a late teen-ager coming from a marginal environment it was, all things considered, a satisfactory report.

Again the phone rang. "Mr. Tibbs, please," a masculine voice said.

"This is Mr. Tibbs."

"Bert Furthman, Mr. Tibbs. You're in charge of this case about the boy with the gun?"

"Yes, I am."

"Then maybe I can help, I don't know. I drive for MTA. Last night about nine-thirty I picked up a youngster who might be the one you're after. He came running up to the bus stop just in time to catch me. I thought it was a little late for a kid his size to be out alone, but I assumed he was going home."

"Of course."

"Well, the reason I'm calling you, I picked up a news-cast that said that the boy with the gun is wearing a worn-out red jacket. That's how this boy was dressed. I remember that he was carrying something, I couldn't say what. I let him off near the end of my run — a half a block from where the shooting took place. Where the colored boy was killed, I mean."

"Thank you very much, Mr. Furthman," Virgil said. "I very much appreciate your coming forward." He took down the driver's address and telephone in case it would be necessary to call him as a witness. The information he had supplied was not new, but it did tie up a loose end. Unfortunately it did nothing to help locate Johnny McGuire *now*. As he hung up the phone he hoped that it would ring again as soon as possible. And with good news.

His wish was granted: before another full minute had passed the ring came again. He picked it up and said, "Virgil Tibbs." Then he held his breath.

"Mr. Tibbs," the voice of Maggie McGuire came tearfully over the line, "I've heard from Johnny!"

He opened his mouth to ask, "Where is he?" and was rescued by his intelligence. "Is he all right?" he asked instead.

"Yes, I think so. He called me on the telephone."

Tibbs raised his hand to get his partner's attention. Bob immediately picked up his own phone. "Did he say where he was, Mrs. McGuire?"

A suppressed sob came over the line. "No, he didn't. I asked him and he said something like, 'I'm here in the phone booth.' That's all."

"Did he say anything else, Mrs. McGuire? Anything at all?"

Maggie did not appear to hear the question for a moment. "I don't know where he slept last night, or what he's had to eat. . . . I'm sorry, you asked me something?"

"Did Johnny tell you anything else at all, Mrs. McGuire?"

For a few seconds there was no answer, then he changed his question. "Please tell me about it, just as it happened."

"Well, I answered the phone and I heard Johnny's voice. He said 'Hello, Mommy.' I remember, just those words."

"Good, go on."

"I . . . I couldn't say anything for a moment, then I think he said something like, 'I'm all right, Mommy.' I'm not sure, I was so upset."

"Of course, Mrs. McGuire, I understand."

"Then I asked him where he was and he said, 'Right here in the phone booth,' like I said. After that he said something about my not worrying. I don't remember what I said to him, I think I said that I would come and get him. Then he told me that his radio was broken."

"Did you reassure him on that?"

"Yes, I told him that we knew and that his father wasn't mad — that's what he would worry about. I told him we knew that it wasn't his fault. Then Johnny said that he was in trouble because he had shot a nigger boy. *Oh, I'm sorry!*"

She burst into tears. Virgil remained silent, letting her take her time. Finally she said, "I'm very sorry. I didn't mean to use that word to you."

"Don't concern yourself about that, Mrs. McGuire, you have enough on your mind. What else did Johnny say?"

She chose her words cautiously. "Well, as I said, Mr. Tibbs, he told me that he had shot the little colored boy. I told him that I didn't care if he did kill him, I wanted him to come home. Of course you understand . . ."

She somehow seemed to sense the reception of her words and stopped. After that, for a moment or two, there was no sound.

"Mrs. McGuire," Virgil began carefully, "I don't want to press you, but did you use that word? Did you tell your son that he *killed* the boy whom he shot?"

"I guess . . . I guess I did." Her voice was very low.

Tibbs could not answer her. He locked his fingers tightly around the telephone. He drew a long breath and fought to keep himself under control. "I'm very sorry that you did that," he said. "So long as Johnny thought that he had just hurt the other boy, there was a good chance that he might have come home to find comfort from you and protection from his father. Now he believes himself to be a murderer. He isn't, of course, but he won't understand that."

"What . . . what are you driving at?" she asked.

"Just this, Mrs. McGuire: I don't want to alarm you, believe me, but in the stricken, desperate frame of mind that he must be in, only God Almighty can say what your son is likely to do now."

10

As soon as Johnny McGuire hung up the phone that had brought him the sound of his mother's voice, he felt his whole body begin to shake and he did not think that his knees would ever again obey his commands. He did manage to pick up his shoe box and walk out of the drugstore onto a busy street of downtown Los Angeles, he did not know which one. Then it seemed to him that he was going to be sick all over the sidewalk.

For a moment he leaned against the solid wall of a building and tried frantically to decide what he should do. What had started out as an adventure and a solution to all of his problems was suddenly reversed; now he was stricken with the realization that he had been traveling farther and farther away from the comfort and security of his home. He had meant to ask his mother if the cops had all gone away; if they had, then he wanted her so much he had all but decided to turn around and try and go home. Now that was impossible, as soon as they found him the cops would shoot him dead.

As he stood there, so utterly alone, he began to think a little more clearly and decided that the cops wouldn't really shoot him on sight, but something terrible would be sure to happen. They were already mad about his father's traffic ticket and what he had done was many times worse.

One thought managed to cut through the confusion in his mind; he could ask Tom Satriano to help him. Mr. Satriano, like all the Angels, lived in Anaheim and therefore he wouldn't have heard about the trouble in Pasadena. The precious letter in his possession would get him in to see him; once in his presence he could tell him about his troubles and the great catcher, who always knew what pitch to call for next, would help him and tell him what to do.

He found new strength in this plan and, at the same time, a fresh resolution not to allow himself to be caught before he reached the stadium. He didn't have his telltale red jacket any more, but he would still have to be very very careful. If he acted like everyone else, then he probably wouldn't be noticed.

From the people passing by he picked out a teen-ager who seemed to be on business of his own and therefore wouldn't stop to ask awkward questions. "Which way is the bus station?" he asked, trying to look self-possessed. The youth turned without stopping. "Fifth and Main," he said and pointed.

That made things easy, Johnny tucked his shoe box under his arm right side up so that the gun could not fall out and then started off at a brisk walk. During the next few minutes no one appeared to take any notice of him: there were too many other people on the streets. He found the station easily and walked inside with a careful show of assurance. He pushed a dollar bill from his small hoard under the wicket and said, "Disneyland."

"Round trip?" The man looked at him a little oddly.

Johnny had not anticipated that question, but he did not dare to panic. "Just one way," he answered. "My dad's meeting me there." His answer seemed to satisfy the ticket seller, but his dollar was not quite enough. Manfully he dug into his pocket and found a few coins. He was on his way to see the Angels and that consideration steeled him against the agony of seeing his precious savings dissipated.

Less than twenty feet from where he stood as he received his ticket a plainclothes officer of the Los Angeles Police Department was casually watching his actions; he had seen Johnny come in alone and in his judgment he was a year or two too young to be on his own. He knew, of course, about the shooting in Pasadena, but the only ID clue he had been given was a worn-out red jacket; he made no connection in his mind, therefore, between the boy he saw buying a ticket and the one for whom the Pasadena police were so frantically searching. Instead he was mildly interested in a boy who just possibly might be trying to run away from home.

Johnny turned and looked about the terminal to see where he might wait without being conspicuous. Then he caught sight of a considerable group of children of his own age and he knew at once what to do. He walked over to them, not too rapidly, and sat down at the end of one of the rows. "Hello," he said to the boy next to him.

"Hello. You going to Disneyland too?"

"Sure." Johnny wiggled back on the seat and tried to look as though he belonged there.

The police officer was satisfied. He had noted the brief interchange and took it for mutual recognition between kids who knew one another even though they weren't pals. He turned his attention back to the station and continued his lookout for any signs of pickups, narcotics violations, or persons who absented themselves for too long an interval in the washrooms.

Johnny McGuire, his shoe box on his lap, sat quietly, content not to push his luck, until the bus was ready to load. Then he rose with all of the others and boarded the vehicle as routinely as possible. He completely fooled the police officer who had given him one more inspection while he had been in line. Instinctively Johnny played the role of a boy properly out for a holiday; the fact that he was apparently carrying his lunch added an authentic touch.

As the bus pulled out he felt a wonderful sense of freedom. He had passed through the most difficult part, all that he had to do now was to sit still until the vehicle he was on took him safely and securely to Anaheim.

In abrupt contrast, tensions were rising sharply in the McGuire home. Less than ten minutes after Maggie had received the call from her son, Mike had burst in the door, hoping for some news. In view of the circumstances, he had been excused from work. When he had been told about the telephone call, he had raged at the traffic delay which had prevented him from getting home in time to receive it himself.

The small apartment was hardly able to contain him as he tried desperately to think of something to do. Mounting worry over his son's whereabouts, and the frustration of forced inaction, had whetted his nerves raw. Twice he picked up the phone to call the police and twice he slammed it back onto its cradle.

Maggie sat silently, afraid to move or utter a sound. She had repeated the phone conversation over and over, three or four times, to the best of her ability until Mike was satisfied that he had extracted every particle of information she had to give. Now he was a caged lion, torn between wanting to go out and search, and the desire to be at home to receive the first bit of additional news that came in.

When the doorbell sounded once briefly, Mike whipped open the only entrance to the apartment and found himself confronting Virgil Tibbs once more. "You found him?" he demanded.

Tibbs shook his head. "Not yet — but we will. I'm glad you're home; I came to ask one or two more questions."

"Come in, then." Once more Mike despised his visitor for his black skin — he desperately wanted a white man to help him, someone he could rely on and trust.

Virgil knew that; he read the tension in the atmosphere as though it had been a newspaper headline. He did not blame the McGuires, they were under a fearful strain and to some degree he shared it with them.

"First of all, every man on the entire police force is helping to look for Johnny," he began. "So are our policewomen. And the people of the city will help, I've already talked to the bus driver who carried him last night."

"How was he?" Maggie asked.

"Just fine at that time. He'll turn up, Mrs. McGuire, he's got to. I'm almost certain we'll have definite news before the day is over."

In response Maggie held out her hand to him, something which for an instant astonished Mike and then, for some reason, made him angry.

"I wanted to ask you," Tibbs said, "where you went to church."

"What's it to you?" Mike snapped.

Virgil turned toward him. "I asked a reasonable enough question, Mr. McGuire; you know that."

"Maybe, but it's none of your goddamned business."

Tibbs tightened slightly, but he kept his own voice under control. "It's very much my business, and you'd know that if you think about it for a minute. Sometimes when children are in trouble, and they're afraid to go home, they'll go instead to a trusted minister — I did."

"Well we don't go to church. Maggie here's a Baptist, but we don't know no ministers out here. Johnny, he wouldn't do that."

Tibbs accepted the answer, then he turned back to his hostess. "Mrs. McGuire, I know you must have gone over your phone conversation with Johnny a hundred times already in your head, and of course you've told Mr. McGuire all about it. Do you think you could repeat it once more for me? There might be some little point you didn't mention when we talked about it."

Wearily Maggie brushed her hair back without being aware of it, swallowed, and once more recited her account of the almost maddeningly limited talk she had had with her son. When she had finished she lowered her head a little, as though ashamed that she had no more to offer.

"And that's all he said."

Maggie nodded, her voice for the moment used up.

"Did you hear any sounds in the background that you might be able to identify? Anything at all?"

Maggie shook her head. "He was in a booth, he said that he was. I didn't hear anything but him."

"If he had only said something more — anything — I might have something to go on."

"He might have said something, if the operator hadn't cut in."

"You said that the operator cut in?"

"Why, yes. The operator came on the line, like they do, and said that three minutes were up and to signal when we were through. So Johnny just said 'good-bye' and hung up."

"There's nothing to that," Mike said.

"Maybe not," Tibbs answered. "On the other hand, it's just possible that it may tell me where to find your son."

11

Fifteen minutes later Virgil Tibbs was in the office of Captain Lindholm, the chief of detectives for the Pasadena Police Department. The chief took one look at his face and waved him to a chair. "You've got something," he said.

"I may have a lead on the McGuire boy, the one with the gun. I put it together out of bits and pieces, but it fits."

"Good. Before you go any farther . . . no, you'd better give me your part first."

"All right, sir, let me lay out the pieces for you. One, the boy has approximately sixteen dollars in his possession, at least he started out with that amount. He must have bought some food somewhere along the line, but it would be from hamburger stands and places like that. Almost impossible to check. Two, he was saving his money to buy a catcher's outfit, for baseball, but in the frame of mind he must be in, I don't think he's buying sports equipment."

"Neither do I," Lindholm agreed.

"Continuing, he is a rabid fan of the California Angels, both because he loves baseball and because he once met Gene Autry. He has a double involvement there; his parents have made that very clear."

"It's a long way to Anaheim, for a boy his age at any rate."

"Agreed, sir, and that's what stopped me, until just a few minutes ago. I know for a fact that he is no longer in Pasadena, at least that was true as of an hour ago."

Lindholm pondered that piece of information. "That does shift the odds, doesn't it."

"Johnny McGuire is only nine years old, but even kids of that age can be remarkably resourceful at times. He's somehow managed to get a bus ride out of town, or possibly hitchhiked, but the probabilities are well against that. Granted that he could have walked all night, but his chances of doing that without being spotted are very slim."

Lindholm shook his head. "He spent the night in the Arroyo Seco, that's what I was going to tell you. I've had two men down there making a thorough search; they found his red jacket rolled up under some bushes."

Virgil was almost afraid to ask the question. "Did they recover the gun?"

"No, they didn't, and once they found the jacket they checked the area very carefully."

"I hope to God he's thrown it away somewhere," Tibbs said.

"Probably he has, but until we can establish it as a fact, we'll have to assume that he's still armed. However, you say he's out of town — how did you get that?"

"He called his mother on the phone to tell her he was all right. The operator cut in to tell him that his three minutes were up. They don't do that on local calls, only those where toll charges are involved."

"About the only place he could go from here by public transportation is into L.A. I'll alert them immediately."

"I'd suggest also, sir, that you advise Anaheim and particularly the security people at the stadium. One boy going to the ball game won't be easy to find, but a boy alone by himself could be a little easier."

"You think he'll get that far?"

Virgil shook his head. "You'll have to polish your own crystal ball on that one. A lot funnier things than that have happened."

Lindholm sat up. "Agreed, except that if he's still got his gun with him, things may not be especially funny before they're over." He looked up. "Yes?"

Virgil turned to find Bob Nakamura behind him. "Something is starting in Brookside Park," Bob reported. "At first it didn't look like much, but it's snowballing."

"Is anybody we know leading it?" Lindholm asked.

"I don't think so, sir, it appears to be more of a spontaneous thing, but it seems to be developing pretty rapidly. Five different patrol cars have called in during the last ten minutes to report a mass movement in that direction. All Negro, but apparently not the hippy types. So far five incidents of rock throwing damage, two store windows broken."

Lindholm quickly picked up the phone. "I'll tell the chief. Virgil, I sent Ted Rasmussen down there, but he's new in his rank and may need some help. You'd better get down there and lend a hand. Call if you need more manpower. As soon as I talk to Chief Addis I'll call Anaheim." He dialed.

"Yes, sir," Tibbs answered and left.

Sergeant Ted Rasmussen set his jaw hard and resolved to do his duty, no matter what. In the back of the station wagon he was driving there was a mobile command post which would enable him to direct the five other men assigned to him, or to communicate with headquarters if necessary.

Brookside Park was the trouble area of Pasadena, he knew that well although almost all of his work to date had been in the field of traffic. Any problems involving moving vehicles he could handle; what he was up against now was something else, but he would have to hack it because the responsibility was his.

A swiftly thrown rock hit hard against the right front fender of his police car. He took no responsive action; he was needed where he was going and he had no time for a probably futile chase on foot of some leggy teen-ager. When he passed a car parked at the curb which had a freshly broken windshield he ignored it too. Ahead of him lay a much greater ugliness.

Essentially a quiet man, Ted Rasmussen was depending on the authority of the law, and the training he had received for his new job, to handle the situation. He knew quite a bit about riots; he had seen a graphic news photo of a policeman, his face streaming blood, who had been caught in the melee of a New Jersey uprising. The memory of that picture steeled him; what had to be done, he would do.

As he neared the park he was surprised by the number of parked vehicles; he guessed immediately that at least some of them had brought people from Los Angeles. Some of them would have come just to see the excitement; others might well be hard-core militants who were ripe for hostile action.

His first glimpse of the crowd which had already gathered hit him like a blow in the abdomen; he had not expected half that many. One quick look around the area told him that more people were streaming in on foot, some even running.

On a raised platform a speaker was haranguing the crowd. He had a loudspeaker system which he was using to augment the natural power of his voice. In the first few words that he caught Rasmussen heard the speaker talking about what a wonderful boy Willie Orthcutt had been.

Ted Rasmussen pulled his station wagon up behind the gathering crowd of listeners and went around immediately to set up his command post. He dropped the tail gate, flipped on the switches of the electronic equipment, then turned to the two men who had been riding with him. "You know what to do," he said crisply. "Go to the far side of the crowd and stay there. If I have to make an announcement, I want you to be able to testify that it was audible at the furthest point. Keep out of trouble if you can; if you need help, let me know fast."

The two uniformed officers left together, walking rapidly around the perimeter of the growing mass of humanity. Behind the sergeant the car which had come with him unloaded three more uniformed men.

The police had made great strides in crowd handling since the outbreak of violence in Watts a few years previously and the sergeant had been well briefed. "You had better keep your batons with you. Don't make a show of them, but if it becomes a question of self-protection, then do whatever is necessary. Avoid an incident if you possibly can." He nodded toward the speaker. "I don't know who that man is, but so long as he confines himself to protest, demanding Negro rights, and things like that, he's within the law. Remember that. If he gets out of line to the point where we'll have to take action, then I'll let you know. Now spread out a little, but keep me in sight."

The three officers followed instructions; it was a case now where their uniforms were their best protection. Although they were armed, against a mob of hundreds, if the crowd broke loose, they would be virtually helpless.

Ted Rasmussen tapped his fingernail against the public address microphone and verified the fact that the system in his station wagon was in working order. Then he picked up his communications mike and reported that he was on the job and had made his initial deployment. He was not able to give an accurate estimate of the size of the crowd, but he asked for reinforcements on the basis of the outsider cars he had spotted while driving in.

He had barely pressed the mike back into its clip when a youth darted out of the crowd, aimed a rock at one of the uniformed men, and then scurried back into the jam of people. Fortunately he missed; Rasmussen saw it and signaled his men not to give pursuit. He tried to sense the feeling of the crowd, the extent to which it had been aroused, and he was not sure of his result. The speaker was well launched into a poignant description and biography of the dead Orthcutt boy; the crowd was responding, but everything that came out of the loudspeakers was well within the law.

The communications set came alive with the message that another six uniformed men were being dispatched. Also Virgil Tibbs was on his way and should arrive at any moment. That was good news for Rasmussen; if things got any worse, Virgil, being both experienced and a Negro, could be a real help.

"An' I ask you, are we goin' to let them do that to *us*?" The sudden increase in the power of the speaker's voice awoke Rasmussen to the fact that he had not been listening and that something had been said which he should have heard. A roar of response came from the crowd, and with it a wave of movement. An unmarked car drew up behind the station wagon and Tibbs got out.

"We pay our taxes in Pasadena, but we ain't *citizens* of Pasadena," the speaker went on. "You know this is a rich man's playground, but it's rich *white* men! Every year they crown a pretty *white* Rose Queen an' have big parties while we're crowded into ghettos. And that ain't right!"

"Know him?" Rasmussen asked Tibbs.

Virgil shook his head. "He's not one of the Negro community leaders, he could be from outside, or just someone who wants to sound off."

The crowd reaction was mounting, the speaker sensed it, and he responded in turn. The sense of caution which he had been evidencing began to vanish; his words took on a new bite and any sense of restraint was swept away.

"This town is a symbol of the white man's world, the white man's *dying* world. He ain't goin' to be in charge much longer. This boy, this Willie Orthcutt: I'm telling you he was *better* than any white kid in this here whole town. And who killed him? *A white boy killed him.* A sneering white boy pointed a gun at poor, unarmed Willie, pointed it right at his guts and shot him dead. He didn't even know him, but he shot him dead because he was black!"

A wave of ugly sound ran through the crowd. Rasmussen looked at Tibbs quickly, searching his face for a clue as to what he should do. Virgil revealed no expression at all, he was simply listening intently to the speaker's words.

The speaker paused and read his audience. There was

a steady stirring now, an undercurrent of mounting tension which charged the air. He had his listeners with him and he knew it. Suddenly he felt the power; understood that if he were bold enough, he could rouse the people before him into action. He drew a deep breath and made his gamble.

"Well, are we just gonna stand here and talk about it, or are we gonna *do* something? It's time they were *afraid* of us, it's been the other way too long. I say that we go now, like they did in Watts, and give 'em hell until every brown-nosed cop gets down on his knees out of FEAR every time he sees a black man's face!!"

Virgil thrust the public address microphone into Rasmussen's hands. "That does it," he said abruptly. "Put out the riot act — fast."

Rasmussen gulped air and held the microphone before his lips. "This is Sergeant Rasmussen speaking," he declared. "I am a peace officer of the State of California and of the City of Pasadena. I declare this to be an unlawful assembly and command you in the name of the people of this state to disperse immediately. All those remaining present will be subject to arrest."

The speaker heard and understood the formal words, but he had worked himself into such a condition that he no longer cared. "An' is it lawful," he roared back, "to commit cold-blooded murder? You go catch that white boy and leave us alone."

"Take care of your men," Tibbs said. "I'm going in after him."

"No!" Rasmussen said.

Virgil laid a quick hand on his shoulder. "Thanks, Ted, but in my case it's different — I've got a black face. Stand by."

He began to weave his way into the mob. As he worked forward he heard the speaker's voice cutting through the air. "Now there's a white man back there who says that we all gotta go away. Just because *he* said so. Have we got rights, or haven't we?"

As he worked forward as fast as he could, Virgil Tibbs tried to understand what the speaker was feeling. Raw in his own mind were memories of his childhood in the deep South when he had been called a pickaninny among other things, of his growing years when he had had to be afraid, particularly at night, of cars filled with three or four young white men just because he had a black skin. He remembered bitterly the hundreds of times he had been made to step off the sidewalk because a white man wanted to pass and then he could see himself in the position of the man who was still talking, seeking to escape from the trap into which his racial heritage had thrust him.

As he moved he tried to block out of his mind the risk he was taking, and the limited chance that he would come out of this rebellious crowd with both the man he was after and a whole skin.

He wormed through the tightly packed front row of listeners, walked to the side, and climbed up onto the small platform from which the speaker was still talking. His voice was beginning to fail him now and a decided hoarseness tinged his words. When he sensed that he was no longer alone, he turned, faced Tibbs, and said, "Whadda *you* want?"

"I'll take over," Virgil said. "Your voice is gone."

"You think you can?"

"Damn right." Without knowing yet what he was going to say Virgil Tibbs took over the microphone and faced the crowd. He sensed at once that to reason would be out of the question; he would have to pick up where the other man had left off and somehow direct things from there.

He raised his own voice, therefore, and deliberately put a bite into it. "How many of you come from Mississippi?" he demanded.

He got a small wave of response.

"Alabama?"

Some hands shot up, some voices answered.

"Georgia?"

Again, a limited reaction.

"Well that's where I come from. That's where we locked the doors nights, not because we had anything worth stealing, but because we were afraid of white men."

A bigger reaction this time — a swelling volume of sound and motion.

"I know what it means, brother," Virgil went on, "because I've been there! I washed cars for three years and saved my money so I could come to California. I heard I could go to school here and they'd let me. I wanted to come; we lived in a shack where my mother cooked our food, when we were lucky enough to have any, over a wood stove. A white man built the house for us colored to live in and he didn't bother to put in any bathroom."

They were listening to him now. Very few who heard his words had any idea who he was, but they knew that he had taken command in a decisive manner, and that he was black. So they waited to find out what he would do or say next.

"Willie Orthcutt was a wonderful boy," Tibbs went on. "I never met him, but I know all about him and I can tell you this — he would have made his mark in the world."

He leaned forward until the tension now in his being could be seen and felt. "I don't know the white boy who shot Willie Orthcutt, but I'll promise you something — I'm going to find him. And when I do, justice is going to be done and you can depend on it!"

He was an enigma to the crowd; he was telling them what they wanted to hear, but he was speaking to them with the voice of an educated man — a man who might have been white. He could easily have put a Southern slur into his speech, he had talked that way all through his childhood and had never forgotten how. It had taken him long hard work to overcome it. But he would not do it; he talked to them as he was now and made no apology.

"They did let me into school, as I was promised, and I washed dishes in a fraternity house until I graduated." At that moment he sensed that he must make his move. "Now I'm working for you," he went on without a break. "I'm going to catch that boy; take all the bets you can get on it. I'm a police officer *and that's my job!*"

The man who had been speaking thrust himself forward and took possession of the microphone. "You know who he is?" he demanded. "He's a white man in a black man's skin!"

Before Tibbs could respond to that a youth darted out of the crowd and leaped up onto the platform. He had a fanatical glint in his eye, but he seemed to know what he was doing. Virgil recognized Charles Dempsey. The crowd was on the fence now and it could go either way. He decided to let Dempsey go ahead — because to prevent him from doing so might be fatal.

With a self-possession well beyond his years the teen-ager faced the microphone and the crowd. "Hey," he shouted. "Ya all know me. If ya don't, you heard about me. I'm Sport. You see all these cops around here? Well this here is their boss, *and he's a black man!*"

He swung his arm wide to arrest attention. "*I was there when Willie Orthcutt was killed,*" he yelled at the top of his voice. "*He was with me. I saw the white kid do it. And this here black man's gonna ketch him. He's gonna make that white kid hate the day he was born. Now let 'im go do it!*"

Virgil read the crowd's reaction and quickly took command. "OK," he announced. "The party's over. If you go cool now, no one will get hurt and you won't get arrested."

It didn't quite take, so he resorted to dramatics. Over the microphone he called to Rasmussen. "Call your men back. Let these people through. Let them go home, however they want."

Ted Rasmussen knew, as every experienced police officer does, that acting is sometimes a vital part of law enforcement. He understood at once what Virgil was doing and he used his own public address system to respond. "Whatever you say, sir," he came back.

It was enough. Even amplified the words came out respectful and subservient, as he intended them to. Some of the people sneered at him a little as they began to go past where he was standing, but he did not mind. He was glad to let Virgil take all the bows, he had earned them.

On the platform Tibbs took down the name and address of the speaker and then spoke to him quietly. "I know how you feel," he said. "I've felt that way more times than you can count. But don't ever call me a white man that way again — I'm a Negro, I know it, and I'm proud of it. I had to work two times harder than any white man to get where I am, now don't you try to take it away from me."

"All right," the man said.

Virgil snapped his notebook shut. "You were het up," he went on. "I told you I can understand that. Have you ever been arrested before?"

Worried now, the man shook his head. "Traffic tickets, that's all."

"Then go on home and don't get involved in any mess

like this again. Inciting to riot is a serious charge, you could do time for it."

The ex-speaker decided not to push his luck. "Thanks," he said.

"Good enough. If your record is as clean as you say that it is, then you can forget about today. If it isn't . . ." Tibbs tapped his notebook and then slipped it into his pocket.

The show was over, the crowd was flowing away. When the area had cleared enough Virgil walked calmly back to where the station wagon was still standing and said, "Let's go."

On the way back into his office Tibbs encountered Captain Lindholm in the corridor. "I heard what happened," the captain told him. "You did a good job. Now please get back onto that problem about the McGuire boy before something a lot worse happens. Try to get that youngster back today if you can — take him into protective custody if you have to. Get the gun away from him. I know what I'm asking, but there isn't any alternative."

"I'll do my best," Virgil promised, and went to his desk. Before he could sit down Bob Nakamura intercepted him and indicated that he had some news.

"I've got a lead for you. While you were out a call came in from a filling station attendant who works nights near Orange Grove Avenue. He had just gotten out of bed and heard a newscast. He phoned in to say that a boy of about nine or so, who looked as though he might have been out all night, came in and asked to use the washroom about six this morning. He didn't have a red jacket, but he was carrying a shoe box."

"A shoe box?"

"Yes, now get this: after he used the head he asked for directions to Anaheim, by road and by bus. He said that his father was going to take him there. The attendant briefed him and gave him a map. When he asked the boy why he was up so early, he said that he had a paper route."

Virgil nodded, thinking as he did so. "That was Johnny all right, and you know what was in the shoe box. Anaheim! It fits."

"And Orange Grove is where you catch the bus into L.A."

Tibbs became aware of a visitor and looked up to see Charles Dempsey framed in the doorway.

"I didn't mean to listen, honest I didn't," Sport said.

"Don't worry about it," Virgil answered. "I'm glad you're here, it gives me the chance to thank you for what you did down in the park. I'll mention it in my report."

The young Negro flushed with pride and satisfaction. "You better make me look good now, heh?"

"I'll certainly try." He turned to his partner. "Help me out. Call Anaheim and tell them that I'm coming into their jurisdiction. Kill the jacket ID, it's been recovered, and advise them about the shoe box — that ought to be fairly easy to spot. I'm going over to get the boy's father and take him

141

down there, we may need him before we're through." He looked up sternly at Sport who was still in the doorway. "You heard this accidently, that's understood, but I'm telling you now not to breathe a word about it to anybody, I don't care who he is. Can I trust you?"

Instead of answering the lanky youth spread out his hands in appeal. "Please, can I come with ya? I won't do nothin', but I figure I got that comin'."

Tibbs made a fast decision; he would have given a great deal if the teen-ager had not heard what had been said and he blamed himself for not having been more careful. "I can't take you down in the official car, that's absolutely out. Under no circumstances do I want you to follow me after I leave here — and that's an order. If you want to drive to Anaheim on your own, then that's your privilege."

Bob Nakamura understood perfectly; if Dempsey got in the way down there, Virgil would handle it. "I'll pass the word that you're on your way," he said, then his voice became grim. "Enjoy the ball game."

12

As the bus rolled smoothly down the Santa Ana Free-way, Johnny McGuire sat staring out of the window. He had escaped now from Pasadena, but he knew that within a matter of hours he would have to go back. He was on his way to see the Angels in person and meet Tom Satriano face-to-face, but he was also moving farther and farther away from his mother and father who offered the only real shelter, protection, and love that he had ever known.

The vehicle he was riding in was taking him to Dis-neyland, an almost unbelievable place of enchantment, but so deep was his preoccupation with his troubles, he was hardly aware of that fact. Instead he saw before him, repeated like the rotating patterns of early moving picture devices, the fear-ful image of the boy he had shot. He saw him standing there;

he felt the gun go off in his hand. Then with terrible clarity he saw the boy fold his arms across his abdomen and slump to the ground.

He, Johnny, had done that terrible thing with his father's gun. And what was the worst part, he could not say that he was sorry and help the boy to get up again. A horrible, ice-cold chill seized him as he realized once again the paralyzing fact that the boy was dead. His mother had told him so — he had killed the nigger boy.

His chest began to tighten and he wanted to cry. If he could have done so, he would have gotten off the bus right then and started back to Pasadena, back to his mother who would shelter him. He was ready to face the punishment he knew he would have to accept, from the cops for killing the boy and from his father for breaking his radio and then running away. The radio part was not too bad, his mother had told him that his father knew that it had not been his fault. But he had taken his radio to school and he knew that that had been wrong. It had started the whole thing.

The bus edged into the right hand lane, went up an exit ramp, and turned right onto a main surface artery. Towering before him he saw the mighty form of the Matterhorn. Presently the slim outline of a rocket poised on its pad came into view and he knew that this was indeed the magic kingdom, the fabulous Disneyland. But even more than that, it meant that he was in Anaheim!

The gas station man had told him that the Angels baseball stadium was less than a mile away. Excitement began to build up within him. This might be his last day before he would have to go to prison, but this one precious day would be the greatest one of his life.

The bus turned off the highway into the immense Disneyland parking lot. Overhead a helicopter was just settling down onto the pad provided for air travelers. Up on an embankment an enthralling, old-fashioned steam engine was slowly pulling a string of cars into a station. The bus drove up before the main ticket gates and stopped.

Johnny tried hard to think, to decide what he should do. He did not have a watch, but he knew that it was still midmorning and that the baseball park would not yet be open. He would have been content just to go there and sit, looking at the stadium, but that would invite notice and he knew that he must keep himself concealed in the crowd.

There was only one thing to do, to go into Disneyland and wait there until the ball park would be open. There were a great many cars already on the parking lot; that meant there would be a lot of people inside and he would not be conspicuous.

The others on the bus were already on their feet, eager to be out and on their way through the gates. Johnny joined them, his shoe box tucked under his arm, his hand in his pocket to make sure that his precious money was still safe. At that moment the thought came to him that there would probably be a clock in Disneyland which he could watch to see when he should leave.

While waiting in line at the ticket window, he considered the various combinations offered. His first thought was to buy admission only, but his protective instinct told him that that would be an unnatural thing to do — it would be noticed. The more elaborate offerings were out of the question, he would not have the time and they cost far too much. He decided on the lowest-priced combination ticket as a logical purchase and one which would conserve his resources as much as he dared. When it was his turn he pushed four dollars under the window and received his book of coupons. His shoe box got in the way as he tried to pick up his change and the tickets at the same time; at last he succeeded and made his way to the entrance turnstile. He passed inside without further trouble, walked through the tunnel under the railroad tracks, and found himself in nineteenth century America.

Then he began to worry about his gun. He did not dare to hide it anywhere, someone might find it, but if he carried it with him, then sooner or later it might fall out of its box if he were riding on something. The town hall on his left attracted him; he walked toward it until he saw the small, coin-operated lockers where packages and purchases could be stored. His heart leaped a little; he would have to spend some more money, but his gun would be safe and away from suspicious eyes. Carefully he pushed his shoe box into one of the cubicles, deposited a quarter, and withdrew the key. Now his problem was solved, he was free for the first time in eighteen hours from the burden of his accursed gun, now he could safely explore the wonders of Disneyland.

With his book of tickets in his hand he began to walk up the main street toward the great central plaza where Frontierland, Adventureland, Fantasyland, Tomorrowland, and all the other miracles awaited him. He was just a boy now, exactly like thousands of other boys who already were spread out across the great amusement park. He would have been almost as hard to find as a single ripening ear in a vast cornfield, but it made no difference because in that place, at that time, no one had as yet heard of Johnny McGuire.

During the next two hours he had one of the greatest times of his life. He spent one of his precious E tickets on the Pirates of the Caribbean and was overwhelmed by the adventure. After that great experience he wandered around for the next few minutes, just seeing all of the things about him. Then with one of his lower value tickets he rode the huge merry-go-round and as he did so wished fervently that he could be free to return to this wonderful place over and over again with his father and mother so that they could ride the merry-go-round too.

Because he knew that he would never be coming back again, at least not until after he had spent his time in prison, he used up all of his limited supply of tickets. The submarine he rode revealed to him a totally new and unbelievable world. He wanted to ride the bobsleds on the Matterhorn, but he had no ticket left that would admit him to that high-priced attraction.

In his last few minutes he went back to Frontierland

to drink in all of its wonders and to look once again at the mighty Mississippi River steamboat which arrived and departed with grandeur every few minutes. He had no ticket to ride it, but it was a wonderful spectacle just to see. After he had watched it sail once more he turned and began to walk down the wooden plank sidewalk toward the central plaza. As he passed by the Western store he paused and studied the many things it had to offer, for each one of them reminded him of Gene Autry, the greatest cowboy who had ever lived, and who had once held out his hand to Johnny McGuire.

The wide door was open and the steady flow of traffic in and out encouraged him to venture inside. He surveyed the merchandise with the utmost care, automatically rejecting those items which cost many dollars, and studying those which cost little. He had no real intention of buying, but there might possibly be some little thing which could actually be his. . . .

He found his heart's desire when he saw what appeared to be a real cowboy hat and which was only two dollars. It was not as large or as fine as many of the others in the store, but it was a real Western hat and white, just like the one Gene Autry wore. He thought about the hat, about how he would love to own it, and about the modest supply of funds he still had in his possession. He had already spent more than a dollar for food and almost two dollars to get to Anaheim, that meant that he had thirteen dollars now. Then, suddenly, he remembered two more things — the money he had spent to get into Disneyland and the fare that he would have to pay to get back home. That cut his resources down to about seven dollars. He completely forgot about the money he had put into the pay telephone and the coin locker where he had concealed his gun.

He guessed that it would cost two dollars to get into the baseball stadium; if he allowed himself one more dollar for food, then he had four dollars left. The hat would cost half that.

"Can I help you, son?"

It was unexpected and for a moment Johnny was badly startled; then he looked up at the man who had spoken to him and saw that he was a cowboy all dressed in his Western clothes. "I was looking at the hat," he said.

With a flourish the clerk took the treasure off the peg, creased it in the proper Western style and carefully fitted it onto Johnny's head. "Now go look at yourself in the mirror," he invited.

Johnny did as he was told and saw himself in a wonderful new light. The boys would never laugh at him at school if he wore this superb hat which marked him as a real cowboy; even Billy Hotchkiss would be impressed and at last treat him as an equal. After the cowboy salesman had creased it for him and put it on his head it would have to be his; he could not possibly tell a man like that that it was beyond his means.

"How do you like it?" the clerk asked.

"It's wonderful," Johnny admitted.

"Would you like to buy it?"

It was a fair question with no hint of pressure behind it. Johnny drew breath to announce his important decision when he looked into the case before him and saw a gun belt. He stared at it so hard that the clerk obligingly removed it and squatting down fitted it around Johnny's waist. "There," he said. "Now you're a real cowboy and no mistake."

"How much is it?" Johnny said.

"Two-fifty complete with the gun. It's a regular six shooter, see." The clerk removed the cap pistol and for a fascinating few seconds twirled it expertly in his fingers.

"I've got a gun," Johnny said.

The clerk looked at him. "Then you've got a belt too, haven't you?"

"No, sir."

"Would you like one?"

"How much does it cost?" Johnny asked.

The clerk surveyed him carefully, looked at his shoes, at the worn knees of his pants, and then thought for a second. "Well, the belts and guns come together as a set. But it just happens that I have a belt left over, somebody swiped the gun when I wasn't looking. If you buy the hat, I'll give you the belt for fifty cents."

Johnny could not believe his wonderful luck; it came to him that this was a real cowboy and that was why he was being so generous and good to him. "I'll take it," he said quickly, before the offer could be revoked.

"All right, son, fine, that will be two-sixty-three with the tax."

"Yes, sir," Johnny said. Almost holding his breath he dug into his pocket and pulled out his little stock of bills. He carefully parted with two paper dollars and from his change counted out sixty-five cents. The clerk rang the register and gave him a receipt together with two cents change. "All right, son, have a good time."

In his splendid new regalia Johnny hurried out of the store, for the moment so proud that the horror of the night before was banished from his mind. Then he looked at a clock and saw that it was past eleven; it was time to go to the baseball park.

As fast as he dared he hurried down the main street, past all of the wonderfully inviting stores, and to the town hall lockers where he had left his shoe box. Mercifully, no one else was there at the moment. With some labor he fished out the locker key, inserted it, and swung the small steel door open. There was his precious cache, just as he had left it.

He looked carefully both ways — no one seemed to be paying him the least attention. With a coolness that a professional gambler would have admired, Johnny opened the box, took out his gun, and fitted it experimentally into the holster he had just purchased. The neat little Chief's Special snuggled into the pocket as though they had been designed for each other; it was an almost perfect fit. Greatly relieved that the problem of the awkward shoe box had been solved,

Johnny pushed the box well down into a trash receptacle only a few feet away. With a sense of freedom, and feeling vastly uplifted by his wonderful new possessions, he walked through the tunnel and toward the exit gate, confident now that, somehow, he would find an answer to all of his troubles.

He was halfway through the exit when a man barked at him, "Hey, kid!"

Johnny did not dare to ignore the challenge; his right hand stole toward the butt of his gun as he turned to see what was the matter. "Come here," he directed.

Cautiously Johnny obeyed. He was properly armed now and if there was to be trouble, he knew what to do. As he came closer the man reached out. "Give me your hand," he said.

With his eyes narrowed and worried Johnny carefully offered his left hand, his right resting on the butt of his reliable weapon.

The man took a stamp and pressed it against Johnny's flesh. "There," he explained. "That'll let you back in again. Be sure to come to this gate." Still holding Johnny's hand he moved it under an ultraviolet light; immediately the pattern of the stamp became visible in a pale glowing tint.

As the shadow of danger passed, Johnny made a quick decision. "Do you know where the ball park is?" he asked.

"Sure." The man pointed. "Right over there, cross the freeway and you can't miss it."

"Thanks."

"That's all right. Have a nice time."

"Yes, sir."

Johnny walked away from the gate at a carefully controlled pace; within a minute he was able to slip through the first of the solid rows of parked cars and out of sight of people who might wonder why he was leaving so soon. It was a long way to the gate where the bus had driven in, but when he reached it there was no problem. He walked out calmly and was not challenged. Turning left as he had been directed, he began his hike to the baseball park.

Ten minutes later the Disneyland security office received the first word to be on the alert for an unaccompanied nine-year-old boy who would be carrying a shoe box. When the situation was made clear word was spread quickly to the gatekeepers and to all of the members of the protective force. Very shortly after Disneyland had been notified the police stationed in and around the Anaheim stadium received the same message; within minutes all of the ticket sellers, gatemen, and ushers were cautioned and forewarned.

In the bright sun of the warm day Johnny McGuire walked along the side of the highway feeling just a little lonely, but so proud of his comfortable new hat that he was able to put certain other worrisome thoughts out of his mind. He managed to forget that his stock of money, which had seemed so ample when he had started out, was melting away with distressing speed. His next purchase would be a ticket to get into the baseball park, then he planned to buy himself a hot dog for lunch. Beyond that point he did not attempt to go.

A car slowed beside him and the driver leaned over. "Where are you headed, cowboy?" he asked.

"I'm going to the ball game," Johnny answered truthfully.

"Hop in, I'll give you a lift."

Johnny's mother had cautioned him about accepting rides from strangers, but that had been under different circumstances. Without hesitation Johnny accepted the offered hospitality; he ducked so that his new hat would not be knocked off and carefully shut the door when he was inside.

"Are you an Angel fan?" the driver asked.

"Yes, sir!" Johnny declared.

"Who's your favorite player?"

"Tom Satriano, I think he's great."

"He's a very good catcher. Do you go to the game often?"

Johnny thought very fast before he answered that one. "No, sir, this is the first time that my dad has let me go."

The driver did not comment; it is doubtful if Johnny would have heard him had he done so, because at that moment the car was crossing over the freeway and there before him Johnny saw the great curved shape of the Anaheim stadium.

They drove down a wide roadway, then turned right into another and there, almost at once, were the gates to the parking lot. Johnny was startled that it cost a whole dollar just to drive in; he even felt a certain sense of guilt as though he had somehow brought it about. The driver did not seem to mind: he continued down through the parking lot to a vacant location reasonably close to the main entrance and then stopped the car.

"Thank you very much," Johnny said.

"You're welcome. It's nice to meet a boy who has been trained to be polite. What's your name?"

"Johnny." He said it before he stopped to think.

"Enjoy the game, Johnny. Have you money for your ticket?"

"Yes, sir. Thank you." He got out of the car intent on making his escape because now the man knew his name. He was not sure where he should go, but as he walked closer to the huge stadium he was certain that he would somehow find out how to buy a ticket and get inside. He had been to baseball games once or twice before, but that had been in small wooden grandstands which did not compare with what was before him now.

Keeping his eyes open he watched for the pattern of traffic. It was still early and not too many people had as yet arrived. Although he knew that he was now in Anaheim, far from Pasadena where the police were looking for him, he was also dangerously far from home. If some guard were to notice that he was alone, he might ask some very bad questions. It would be safest, therefore, to do as he had been doing and keep in the crowd as much as possible.

He began to walk around the perimeter to the right,

he could sense that there was more activity in that direction. Ticket windows came into view and Johnny discovered that, as in Disneyland, there were different prices. The first sign he saw was $3.50 and his heart quickened; that was far more than he could afford. Then he saw some windows marked $2.50 and felt that he had saved a whole dollar already. He walked on, anxious to see everything before he invested his money in a possible mistake.

Presently he saw a scattering of boys. As he continued to walk around the sweeping curvature of the stadium he found that there was a large gathering of boys, and some girls too, many older than himself and some of his own age. He knew immediately that here was where he belonged. He hurried to join the crowd which, he saw, was being slowly filtered through two gates into the ball park. Most of the others had small cards in their hands. By looking at two or three of them which were being held in different ways he was able to make out the words "Junior Angels." He did not have a card, of course, but he slowly worked his way up to the entrance just the same. He had his money and in some way he hoped that he could get in.

Then he was funneled into a single line, the boy ahead of him went through, and it was his turn. "Got your pass?" The gateman asked.

Johnny turned a properly stricken face up to him. "I'm sorry, sir," he explained, "I forgot to bring it."

For a moment the man hesitated, then he waved him

through. Immensely grateful for this wonderful and unexpected blessing from heaven, Johnny passed inside and walked toward the ramp to which an usher was directing the traffic. He turned, looked, and saw the playing field, the perfectly kept base paths, the many vast tiers of seats, and the whole spectacle of the great baseball park. Towering over it all was the gigantic A-frame with the halo on top, the symbol of the stadium he had seen pictured so many times. An almost violent thrill of fulfillment took hold of him, he had never known such a sensation. On the field players in gray uniforms were casually warming up; the first real big league players he had ever seen.

Confident now that once he was in this wonderful place nothing wrong could happen to him he pulled out his little plastic wallet, extracted the well-worn letter that it contained, and with it in his hand approached the usher. "I've got a letter from Tom Satriano," he announced proudly. "He says that I can come and see him."

Indulgently the stadium man read the brief communication. "All right son, you'll have to go around to the other side," he directed. "The home team clubhouse is over by third base. Go downstairs, through the tunnel, and then ask the guard to direct you from there."

The talisman had worked! With surging anticipation Johnny hurried down the ramp into the concrete interior of the stadium. The tunnel was long and grim, but he knew that it was taking him in the right direction. Twice he became confused and had to orient himself, but at last he stood before the door of the clubhouse, facing the guard who was posted there, ready for his moment of destiny.

He held out the letter. "Please, sir, I'd like to see Tom Satriano."

The guard read the letter, said, "Just a minute," and disappeared inside.

Desperate, anxious moments passed; Johnny hardly dared to breathe for fear that in some way he would upset the delicate balance of the greatly privileged position he was in. As the seconds passed and nothing whatever happened, he could have screamed from sheer inner tension.

Then the door opened and the guard reappeared. Behind him there was a tall, breathtaking figure in a white baseball uniform. As the man turned to close the door behind him Johnny read the electric number 2 and knew that this was absolutely and truly Tom Satriano himself. When his idol turned toward him, he was so overwhelmed he found that he had lost the power of speech.

And then Tom Satriano held out his hand. Silently Johnny took it; as he felt the strong firm fingers he knew a sudden complete revitalization. Here was the man to whom he could give his complete trust.

"Hello there, cowboy."

His voice was just wonderful; his hero was everything that Johnny had so wanted him to be.

"Hello, sir," Johnny managed. "Can I talk to you for just a little bit?"

"I'd like to very much, but I've got to get out onto the field. I tell you what — you come back here after the game and I'll see what I can do. OK?"

"Yes, sir!" Johnny answered.

He knew that no power on earth could hold him from keeping that appointment. He would be there to talk to his wonderful friend, and to ask his advice, even if the stadium itself were to fall down. And if anybody tried to stop him — well, they wouldn't stop him for long, not while he had his gun ready if he needed it.

13

In the small living room of his apartment Mike Mc-Guire sat, clenching and unclenching his hands, trying to fight down a growing sense of rebellion against the inaction which was being forced upon him. He was tired of going to the door every few minutes to see if his son, by some miracle, might be coming up the steps. Once more he considered, and rejected, the idea of calling the Hotchkiss home; they knew that Johnny was missing and if they found out anything, his common sense told him that they would let him know.

He got to his feet and in pure frustration slammed his fist against the wall. Conflicting thoughts battered him. He was fearfully worried about his son, about what further damage he might wreak with the gun in his possession. He hated to remain at home while others did his searching for him, but he did not know what else to do. Simply to go out and walk the streets, looking for Johnny, offered little hope; there was a far better chance of news if he remained near the telephone. When it seemed to him that he could endure no more, when his raging spirit could no longer remain disciplined within his body, the phone rang.

He answered it almost savagely. While Maggie watched with frightened hope, he carried on a brief conversation and then hung up. "That was that colored cop Tibbs," he reported. "He doesn't know yet where Johnny is, but he thinks he may have an idea where he might have gone."

"Where?" Maggie asked wide-eyed.

"He didn't say, he just asked if I wanted to come with him while he checked it out."

"I think you'd better go," Maggie advised. It was a godsend; she was terrified of her husband in his present dangerous mood — he might do anything.

Mike glanced at the stove and then spoke almost mildly. "Got anything to eat?"

Maggie was engulfed by the guilty knowledge that she had not thought to prepare anything for his lunch. Hastily she took a saucepan of soup she had on the stove and poured it out for a first course. She had been keeping it ready for Johnny in case he came home, but she could not think of that now.

Her husband sat down and began to spoon the soup

noisily into his mouth. In the few moments of grace that she had been granted she searched the small refrigerator; it yielded a piece of hard-cooked meat that she was able to slice up into a sandwich. She added mustard, cut the offering into quarters, and added a handful of leftover potato chips. Johnny liked potato chips and she tried to keep some in the house for him when she could.

Mike ate silently, his jaw muscles working with a steady rhythm while he stared at the wall before him. Maggie set a glass of milk before him and then stood back, afraid almost to breathe. She realized that she had not eaten herself, but that could wait until he was safely on his way. For some undefined reason she had never been as frightened of him as she was now.

There was a step outside and a knock on the door. Wiping her hands quickly on her apron, Maggie answered and admitted Virgil Tibbs. The Negro detective was clearly not overconfident, but there was something about him that made her believe in him. His color still disturbed her a little, but his very neatness, and the way in which he carried himself, suggested that there was within him a kind of strength that she desperately needed to help her in her frightened, fearful, and near frantic situation. She knew very little about him, but she was glad that he was a policeman. Perhaps he might be able to bring her son back to her after all.

She wanted to signal him somehow that her husband was not at his best, but the way in which he greeted them both made it clear that he had grasped that immediately. This time he did not offer to sit down, instead he delivered what news he had to give standing up. "I believe that I may have picked up your boy's trail," he said. "I can't be certain, but there is a good chance that he may be on his way to Anaheim."

"To Anaheim?" Maggie asked, not understanding.

"Yes, that's where the California Angels have their baseball stadium."

"But it's a long way, isn't it?"

"Yes, Mrs. McGuire, it certainly is, but there is bus service. We've almost certainly established the fact that Johnny showed up at an all-night filling station early this morning and used the washroom. Then he asked for instructions as to how to get to Anaheim."

"Was he all right?" Maggie asked anxiously.

Before Tibbs could answer Mike cut in. "But he wouldn't go off just to see a ball game like that, not when he'd know that me and his ma would be sitting here worried sick about him!"

"No, sir, I don't think he would. But you told me something last night that may explain his actions. I don't want to go into it now, but I believe that it would be a very good idea if you would come with me to Anaheim. If we find your boy there, he may need his father's comforting presence very much."

Maggie looked at him swiftly, aware quite suddenly that he understood her husband much better than she had expected.

"I'll come," Mike responded. He picked up a sweater

which was across the back of a chair and then looked at his wife. "What if Johnny comes home while we're away?" he asked.

Maggie drew breath, but Virgil answered for her. "If that happens, Mrs. McGuire, call the police department immediately. They'll get in touch with us by radio. I have a set in the car."

Relieved, Maggie saw the two men to the door and watched while they got into the official car parked at the curb below. When she had seen them drive away she returned to the kitchen, carefully opened another can of soup, and put it on the stove over a low flame. If her boy came home, she was not going to let him go hungry a minute longer than necessary. The police would have to arrest him, she understood that, but he was going to get a warm meal first.

The ball game which was underway at Anaheim was going forward with more than usual speed. Both pitchers were effective, which kept the batters coming up to the plate in a steady succession. The defensive play on the part of both California and Detroit was sparkling. By the end of the sixth inning there had been no errors on either side, while Bobby Knoop had definitely saved a run by a sensational play at second base.

As the game progressed, a number of isolated events began to shape themselves into a pattern. On the Santa Ana Freeway Charles Dempsey in his rebuilt car was making all reasonable speed toward Anaheim and the baseball stadium. There were events likely to take place there in which he was vitally interested. The more that he could witness and later describe firsthand, the greater would be the impact he would be able to make upon his return.

A notice to appear in traffic court was mailed to Mike McGuire at his home. At the same time the attorney for the man whose car he had forced into the center freeway divider sent him a stiff letter demanding payment for all damages under threat of an immediate lawsuit.

At Disneyland the security force was on the sharp lookout for a boy carrying a shoe box, or any apparently unaccompanied youngster of the proper age who might be Johnny McGuire. It was considered likely that he might have disposed of his dangerous weapon at some convenient opportunity. In response, an intensive search for it was put on with every possible part of the grounds being combed for the gun. Despite the thoroughness of the effort, it was so skillfully done that literally none of the thousands of visitors who were enjoying the park had any idea that something might be amiss.

Several young boys were spotted who at first seemed to be alone. When no parents or other escorts appeared three of them were quietly questioned. All three were able to establish their identities to the satisfaction of the security personnel concerned. Four shoe boxes were discovered to be in the park; cautious investigation disclosed that two of them contained bona fide lunches, the other two held shoes brought along for the relief of aching feet. At the end of two and a half hours the Disneyland authorities considered it most likely that if the gun was anywhere on the grounds, Johnny McGuire had probably managed to throw it unnoticed into one of the many ponds and waterways which crisscrossed the grounds. If this were the case, then its prompt recovery would be almost impossible.

Then a positive break came through: the Los Angeles Police Department located the off-duty plainclothes officer who had been stationed in the bus depot that morning. He recalled at once having seen a boy, apparently unaccompanied, carrying a shoe box. The boy had purchased a ticket and then joined a group headed for Disneyland. He had not been wearing a red jacket and there had been nothing about him at the time to excite any undue suspicion, other than the fact that he had been briefly alone. He had had none of the earmarks of a runaway.

As soon as this information reached him, Captain Lindholm notified the Anaheim authorities that the probabilities were now strongly increased that Johnny McGuire was in their jurisdiction. The word was immediately passed to the stadium police detachment and to Disneyland, then it was put on the air and an acknowledgment was received from Virgil Tibbs, who was en route near Downey.

Armed with this additional fact, the Disneyland security chief put additional measures into effect. He was considerably concerned that if a child accidently found the gun, and mistook it for a cap pistol, a very serious accident could occur. Apart from the immediate danger, there was also the threat of the damage such an event could do to the park's reputation. As part of the renewed search, a special crew began a recheck of all of the trash and waste receptacles located anywhere on the grounds.

On the Santa Ana Freeway a minor traffic accident temporarily blocked one lane. Immediately cars and trucks began to pile up behind the stalled vehicles as some motorists fought to get around the obstruction while hundreds of others slowed down to a crawl to see what was going on. Caught in this unexpected congestion Virgil Tibbs accepted it as one of the facts of life; Mike McGuire, his passenger, fumed impatiently and had difficulty understanding that the Pasadena police car could not simply make use of the red lights and siren with which it was equipped somehow to force a way through the stalled traffic.

Eighteen minutes later the shoe box was discovered. The intelligent guard who found it realized immediately that it and its contents had undoubtedly been kept in one of the lockers nearby. He was decidedly disappointed that the box did not contain the gun, but the crumpled paper towels which were inside suggested what their purpose might have been. At the security office the box was expertly examined and a faint trace of what might have been gun oil was detected. Disneyland notified the Anaheim police that it was practically certain that Johnny McGuire's shoe box had been recovered, but that no trace of the weapon it had contained had as yet been found. A crew was then dispatched to search the parking lot which was now the most likely place where the gun might have been discarded. In the comparative privacy between the closely parked cars it would have been easy to slide the weapon somewhere out of sight behind a tire. The fact that he had discarded the shoe box pointed to the likelihood that the missing boy was tired of carrying the gun and anxious to dispose of it. How he might have carried it undetected out of the front gate remained an open question.

In the bottom half of the eighth inning the Angel center fielder got a pitch to his liking and lifted it into the bullpen down the left power alley. It was enough to win the game. Eight pitches disposed of the Detroit hitters in the top half of the ninth and the game was over.

With the final out the stadium underwent an almost immediate transformation. A departure message flashed on the huge scoreboard. The organist swung into the exit music which reached every corner of the stands through the powerful public address system. A row of ushers on each side of the field took up stations where they could prevent any enthusiastic fans from running out onto the playing area. A maintenance mechanic unlocked the elevator car on the side of the big A-frame which supported the scoreboard and the angel halo at the summit. As he went back for replacement light bulbs he mixed with the players who had spent the nine innings of the game in the bullpen.

Through the many wide exit gates the thousands of patrons poured out and spread over the extensive, municipally owned parking lot. A steady stream of cars began to line up for the left turn toward the freeway while dozens of officers assigned for the purpose separated the traffic lanes and let each row move a certain amount in turn.

Johnny McGuire took it all in as part of the splendid spectacle of big league baseball; he did not want to miss one bit of what was going on. Against formidable odds he had made his way to Anaheim, he had seen the Angels play, he had seen them win gloriously. No matter what happened now, this could not be taken away from him. And, in a few minutes, he had an appointment to talk with Tom Satriano. That would solve all of his remaining problems, because Tom Satriano would tell him what to do.

From the end of the stands where the Junior Angels had been seated he ran down the ramps full of excitement, then he slowed down a little in order to savor more of the great event which was about to occur. So that he could see all of the ball park, and view it from as many different angles as possible, he remained on the field box level and walked around to the third base side against the flow of thinning traffic. This was different than the route through the tunnels, but he could see more and he was sure that he would be able to find the clubhouse. He stopped when he was squarely in line with the pitcher's mound and home plate to visualize for a moment the wonderful role he would someday play, crouching behind the plate, signaling to the man on the mound, ready to cut down the runner at first if he dared to attempt to steal.

Glowing with the thought of himself as a big league baseball player, he tore himself away and looked for a way down into the tunnel system which led to the players' clubhouse. His attention was diverted for a moment when he saw the small car begin to climb up the side of the scoreboard frame. He hoped to see it go all of the way, but it stopped after only a short distance. The mechanic changed a bulb and then came down again.

When he turned back and found an entrance to the lower level disaster overtook him — an usher was standing squarely in the middle and waving people to the left and to the right. Johnny ran up to him and said, "I've got to see Tom Satriano."

The usher looked down at him and shook his head. "I'm sorry, you aren't allowed down in the clubhouse area. You can see the players after they're dressed; go out back where their cars are parked."

"He's expecting me," Johnny protested. "I made a date with him. He wrote me a letter."

"May I see it, please?"

Johnny reached for his wallet and then was stricken — he remembered that he had given the precious letter to the guard at the clubhouse door. He had taken it inside and it had not been returned. "I don't have it any more," he admitted. "I gave it to the guard downstairs before the game."

"I see. Then the best thing for you to do is to wait back on the parking lot; I can't let you down here now."

Johnny knew that if he tried to bolt past, the usher would catch him; the only solution was to find another entrance. In apparent obedience to the recommendation he had been given he walked away, intent now on letting nothing divert him from his purpose. If he had not stopped to watch the man fixing the sign he could already have been downstairs.

He went all of the way to the end of the left field stands before he found another way to get below. Mercifully, this staircase was not guarded. He walked down step by step to keep his appointment with the man who would help him to overcome all of his problems. He adjusted the angle of his new hat to improve his appearance, made sure of the snug fit of his gun in its holster, and began to walk down the long concrete tunnel which the foresight of the designers had provided. He passed a group of two or three golf carts which were parked in a small alcove as he walked on in the direction which he knew led to the Angels clubhouse.

Meanwhile up above, not far from the main gate, Virgil Tibbs was in a hurried consultation with the sergeant in charge of the stadium police. "I'm damn sorry," the sergeant said. "We had the word out for quite a long time to watch for a boy with a shoe box. Every gateman was on the alert and all of my men on the inside. It's just our hard luck that the game was one of the shortest ones this season — just about two hours."

Virgil pressed his lips together and thought for a moment. "Let's play it this way: the McGuire boy is dead serious about the Angels team, he may try to see some of the players."

"The kids usually wait for them outside," the sergeant advised. "They know where they park their cars."

Tibbs shook his head. "This boy wouldn't know that, he's never been to a major league game before. He might even try to see Gene Autry if he's here."

"Mr. Autry has an office here and, of course, he's got a private box." The sergeant turned toward the phone. "Let me try the clubhouse; I'll see what I can find out there."

Mike McGuire, who had been standing tensely in the background, gave vent to his feelings. "It's that damn accident that held us up. We'd have been all right if that hadn't happened and everybody had to stop and gawk."

Virgil answered him with a nod; he had no intention of wasting critical time with a useless discussion.

The phone conversation with the clubhouse was agonizingly slow, the sergeant leaned heavily on the counter and waited while someone at the other end of the line apparently took twice as long as necessary to do a simple thing. At last there was a response, he listened for a moment and then passed the phone to Tibbs. "Tom Satriano is on the line," he advised. "He may have something for you."

"Tom Satriano of course!" He took the phone in one swift motion, chagrin on his features. "Mr. Satriano, this is Virgil Tibbs of the Pasadena police. What can you tell me?"

"A young boy came to see me before the game; he

had a note that I had written to him some time ago. He must have carried it for weeks. About eight or nine, dressed in a cowboy outfit."

"A cowboy outfit?"

"Yes, at least he had on a cowboy-type hat, the kind that kids like to wear."

"Did it appear to be a new one, Mr. Satriano?"

The catcher thought a moment. "Yes, I'd say so. He seemed like a nice youngster. I couldn't talk to him then, but I told him I'd see him after the game."

"Good! Was he carrying anything — any bag, any sort of a container?"

"No, sir, not that I saw. I'm sure of it because I noticed when I shook hands with him."

"Thank God for that," Virgil said — he could not help himself.

"Why, what was he supposed to have?"

"A gun — a real one. He shot a boy with it last night."

"Wait a minute — I told you this boy had on a cowboy outfit." Satriano's voice was tighter now and more hurried. "I remember now, he had a toy gun belt too."

Tibbs tightened his right hand into a fist and laid it hard on the counter before him. "Did you see a gun, sir?"

"I'm not sure, but I believe that maybe I did."

Virgil swallowed hard. "All right, since you said you'd see the boy after the game, he's almost certain to show up. When he comes back, please welcome him; it's very important.

You are in no danger, sir, I happen to know that he idolizes you. He cut your picture out of the paper and kept it. And he wrote to you. Please, introduce him to some of the other players. Just keep him there, will you do that?"

"Yes, of course."

"Thank you. The boy isn't vicious; the shooting last night wasn't his fault. His part of it was an accident; I'm certain that he never intended to hurt anyone."

"Wait," Satriano cut in, "how's this — I'll invite him to try on my catcher's outfit. He'll have to take off his gun belt to do that."

"That's brilliant," Tibbs said warmly. "The boy's father is here, but I want to keep him out of sight. I'll come right down."

He hung up quickly, then turned to the sergeant. "Tell me how to get to the clubhouse. I'm going alone — just in case."

After he had received directions he turned toward the door, motioning to Mike McGuire to remain where he was. "As soon as we've got your son safely rounded up, I'll send for you," he promised. Then, as he hurried out, he almost fell over the lank form of Charles Dempsey, who was waiting directly outside.

"Need me?" the teen-ager asked, eager willingness shining in his face.

"No, thanks. Go in and lay low. If the boy sees you he might recognize you and panic. He's still got the gun."

With admirable prudence Dempsey obeyed, despite the fact that he had come to see the action and didn't want to miss a bit of it.

Virgil was in no mood to linger, but he still looked around him carefully while he hurried toward the clubhouse. There would not be many boys dressed in cowboy hats in the fast emptying stadium and he might be fortunate enough to spot the one he wanted.

Below him, in the long tunnel under the third base stands, Johnny McGuire felt his heart quickening as he knew that he was coming closer to the clubhouse and the one man who, at that particular moment, was the most important person in his life. Tom Satriano could not be wrong, the very thought was a blasphemy. The fearful burden he had been carrying was already lightening. The happy thought came to him that Tom Satriano would continue to be the first-string catcher for the Angels until he, Johnny McGuire, was grown up and ready to step into his place.

Then, ahead of him, he saw the usher.

It was the same one, the one who had made him go all of the way around just because he had waited a few seconds to watch a light bulb being changed. Instantly the shapeless fears which had been hovering over him all day swooped down upon him once more, as he faced the terrible possibility that he might be prevented from keeping his appointment.

175

The usher was young, hardly more than a teen-ager, but that did not make him any less of a formidable obstacle. Unconsciously Johnny slowed his pace a little, but he kept on coming, hoping for some sort of a reasonable miracle. And then the usher raised his right arm into the air and waved him back.

That shattered the hope that the usher would go away, or simply ignore him. He *had* to get past now; there was no use in trying to find another way. He kept coming steadily forward.

With a maddening display of authority the usher shook his head from side to side. Johnny was hardly more than twenty feet from him now, but he did not stop. His feet slowed in spite of himself, but his determined young spirit would not, and could not, accept defeat.

Then the usher spoke. "I told you that you couldn't come down here. You haven't any right to be in this tunnel. Now go back the way you came."

"No!" Johnny stopped and faced his enemy. "Tom Satriano told me to come and see him after the game."

"Then see him on the parking lot, that's the right place to wait."

Johnny made one desperate effort to be reasonable — to find a happy solution. "Go ask him," he challenged. "He'll tell you. Tell him it's Johnny. He's got the letter he sent me and he's waiting for me now."

The usher rejected it. "Don't tell me what to do, I

know my job. And right now it's keeping kids like you away from the clubhouse. I've got my orders. Now don't make me chase you away or call a policeman."

At that moment, without any delay, Johnny had to make a decision. His mind flashed back to all the white-hatted heroes he had seen on television who, when all else failed, had depended on their reliable weapons. Then that image was immediately blotted out by the picture of the boy he had shot the night before; one more time in his tortured mind he saw him sinking to the ground. He made his decision: he would threaten, but he would not shoot. In the best tradition of the many Westerns he had seen, he drew his gun.

"Let me past," he ordered.

The usher stood there and laughed at him, a mocking laugh that made Johnny hate him with a blazing fury. "You think I'm afraid of that toy gun?" he said. Then he took a menacing step forward.

"It's a real gun," Johnny warned between his tightly clenched teeth.

The usher had had enough, his patience with this troublesome boy ran out. The authority of his uniform had been challenged, and by a belligerent kid who refused to obey a reasonable order. He would not endure that humiliation, it was an affront to the whole organization that he represented. He began to walk calmly forward, to turn the boy around properly and send him on his way.

To Johnny the battle had been joined and there was

no backing away. He was not thinking of Tom Satriano now, only the adversary before him whom he *must* defeat. The usher was bigger, of course, but Johnny knew that he had the weapon. For one frightened instant he hesitated, then he saw that the usher was much closer and would be upon him in a second or two. In that blinding moment, hating the usher as he did, he still remembered the boy he had hit. In a flash the answer came to him — he aimed the gun over his opponent's head, and fired.

Inside the confining tunnel the explosive blast of the shot echoed with total violence. For an instant Johnny thought that his eardrums had been torn from his head; then to his utter amazement he saw the usher fall flat where he had been standing. He did not sink slowly like the boy had done; he dropped like a dead and lifeless thing and lay inert and still.

Then reason departed, the world rocked underneath him, and Johnny lost everything but the raw instinct to survive. With a scream of hysterical fright, he turned and fled.

In the clubhouse close by Tom Satriano heard the sound of the shot and jumped to his feet. In the instant the banter of conversation in the big room froze, for every man there knew about Johnny McGuire and was waiting for him to appear at the door.

Up above, still on the field box level, Virgil Tibbs heard the shot too. He lunged forward and hurtled down the remaining steps, almost throwing himself around the corners.

Back down the long corridor Johnny raced, his gun tightly clenched in his hand, ready now to use it if he had to to clear the path before him. Only the mute concrete bore witness to his flying feet, to the panting of his desperate breath. His new hat flew off and he did not even notice. He was in a frenzy now, a trapped animal running for the first available place that would give him sanctuary.

His lungs pounding with pain, he burst out of the tunnel into the sudden shock of full bright daylight. For a mad, blinding moment he had to stop; he did not know where to go. The gigantic, now empty stadium loomed above and all around him as though it had been designed specifically as a hopeless trap from which no one could escape.

He could never make it across the huge playing area, and if he did there was no place to go when he reached the other side.

The bullpen gate was open; he gulped air into his tortured lungs and bolted through, desperately hoping that there would be a way out on the other side. There was, another gate stood open, but beyond it there was only a great openness, and the concreted banks of a dry river where he could never hope to hide. Then he saw the foot of the towering A-frame and fastened to it the little car provided to lift the maintenance man up all of the way to the ringlike halo that was the symbol of the team and of the stadium itself.

In total desperation Johnny ran for the car and jumped inside. He swung the gate shut which gave him a slight protection and for a few precious seconds studied the simple control mechanism. Then he looked and saw two uniformed policemen running down the third base stands toward him. They were already dangerously near, and they had guns too. His last hesitation disappeared; he pushed the handle and felt the car at once begin to rise under him. It moved very slowly, but fast enough so that he could see the ground falling away and know that for the moment he had taken refuge in something that would give him sanctuary above his enemies.

He reached the base of the scoreboard and watched as the intricate panels moved past him, sinking downward as he rose. Then he looked over the edge and a quick paroxysm of acrophobia seized him. He fought it by looking upward and seeing the great suspended halo much closer than it had been before. The last of the scoreboard moved past and he was on the dizzying height of the overhead structure being carried steadily upward to his doom.

With every bit of courage and self-possession that his spirit would yield, he forced himself to reach for the control. He pushed the handle to the center position. The car stopped.

He was poised now, between heaven and earth. His body began to shake, his knees threatened to unlock, and for a moment blackness began to swirl before his eyes.

14

At close to a dead run Virgil Tibbs tried to follow the sound of the shot, but in the hard-faced tunnels and corridors under the stadium the noise echoed back and forth from a dozen different directions. Other people erupted onto the scene, players still in uniform, a man in a business suit, two anxious policemen. They converged on the spot where the usher still lay face down in the tunnel. The Angel trainer, clad in white, arrived on the run carrying a first aid kit. Two other men, bearing a folded stretcher, were close behind him.

As the trainer began to run expert hands over the man on the floor, the usher began slowly to come to life. He raised himself on his hands and knees, shook his head as though to clear it of disbelief, and then with the trainer's assistance managed to get to his feet.

"Are you all right?" the man in the business suit demanded anxiously.

The usher rubbed the sides of his face with the palms of his hands. "I . . . I guess so." His knees were visibly shaking; the trainer broke a capsule and held it under his nose.

"What happened?"

The pungent fumes from the capsule helped the man to recover himself. "A kid shot at me."

"Where is he?"

"He ran away."

"What happened? Tell us." There was urgency in the businessman's voice.

"Well, first I saw this kid up above. He wanted to come down here and I told him it wasn't allowed. Then, when I came down here myself, he showed up again, coming down the tunnel." He nodded to indicate the direction.

"Go on, don't waste time."

"Like I said, this kid came walking down the corridor. He wanted to go to the clubhouse; he said something about Tom Satriano."

Virgil clenched his teeth in frustration, then he listened as the man went on.

"I told him he couldn't, then the kid got ugly. He had on a cowboy suit. He drew what I thought was a toy gun and threatened me with it. I walked right up to him and then he fired; the gun was real and I don't know how he missed me. I hit the deck and the kid ran. That's all."

"Was he aiming at you, as far as you could tell, when the gun went off?" Tibbs asked.

"Right at me. Like I said, I don't know how he missed."

The sergeant in charge of the stadium police hurried up, closely followed by a tense Mike McGuire. "The boy," the sergeant said. "He's up on the big A. The maintenance car was unlocked. He got into it. We can't control it from down here, but my men'll handle it."

"No!" Mike McGuire's voice cut with a sharp edge. "You might hurt him. Leave it to me."

Virgil spoke then, quietly, but with conviction. "If you don't mind, I'd like to take over: this is a rather special case." He looked at the sergeant. "I don't know your name."

"Wilson."

"Sergeant Wilson, I know that this is your responsibility, but I know quite a lot about that boy and I think that I understand him."

The man in the business suit interrupted. "May I ask who you are?"

"Virgil Tibbs, Pasadena police. This boy is our problem, it's my case."

"Ted Bowsfield, Virgil, I'm stadium manager for the Angels."

Tibbs nodded his acknowledgment to save time. "The boy isn't dangerous, the account that your usher just gave you isn't entirely correct. I realize, of course, that he's been badly frightened. I think I can get the boy to come down and resolve all this."

"Then go ahead, we'll help you all we can."

Virgil did not wait for any more; he ran quickly up the stairs to the field box level, focused his attention on the scoreboard and its towering supporting frame, and took in the whole situation at a glance. Then he went back down immediately to confer with Wilson. "We've got a little time," he said. "For the moment the boy isn't going anywhere, at least I hope to heaven he isn't."

"I'm with you."

"All right. First of all, please get your uniformed men out of sight of the boy, it may lessen his tension a little. Have somebody stand by the power cutoff for that car and set up a line of communication so that we can get word to him quickly if we have to."

"Good. What else?"

"I'd like a thorough check of the tunnel, the boy may have thrown away his gun while he was running. I'll cover the area outside."

Mike McGuire seized Tibbs by the arm. "While you're talking my boy is in danger. Someone's got to climb up there and help him. I'll do it, he won't shoot me." He let go his hold and started down the tunnel; after a step or two he broke into a run. Virgil paced him until they both burst out into the sharp sunlight. Against the glare of the high bright sky Mike pulled up, and shuddered. Then he formed a megaphone with his hands and before Tibbs could stop him called up. "Hang on, son. I'll come and help you!"

A thin, terror-racked voice came down from the car high above. "Don't, Daddy, don't!" The words ended in a hysterical sob.

Mike felt a strong hand on his shoulder, turned, and looked into the dark face close to his. "You're a brave man, Mr. McGuire," Virgil said, "but don't try it, not now. Johnny is completely terrified; if you try to help him, he might do anything."

Mike stood, his head tipped far back, staring at the high perch where his son was isolated.

"We've got to calm him down — to let the fright and terror drain out of him."

McGuire's body shook with suppressed emotion. "But somebody's got to climb up there and save him . . . I'm his father."

"I know, but that doesn't make you a steeplejack. When Johnny calms down, I think we can persuade him to come down by himself. In that way no one will be hurt. It will mean a great deal to him that you're here to welcome him. But if he had the idea, even for a moment, that you were coming up to punish him . . ." He left the sentence unfinished.

"Then what do we *do*?"

Virgil looked at him. "I suggest that you sit in the stands — close by. I've got an idea that might work. But I can't try it with you here."

Mike gathered himself and clenched his fists. It was hard for him, almost beyond the power of his self-discipline, but he finally gained control over himself. Slowly, and reluctantly, he walked to the railing at the edge of the field. He climbed over and then sat down in the front row.

Tibbs returned to the entrance to the tunnel to find a tall, well set-up man in an Angel uniform waiting there. "I'm Tom Satriano," he said. "Can I help?"

"Yes," Virgil answered, "you can. How many of the players are still in uniform?"

"Most of the crew. Fifteen or twenty."

"Do you think they would be willing to help out?"

"Of course; that's why we waited."

"Then here's what I'd like to ask, and I know it's an imposition. Would some of you be willing to come out here and start a little action in the general area of the scoreboard? As though you were warming up for a game."

"I've got it," Satriano said, turned, and ran with a professional athlete's skill down the tunnel. In less than two minutes players began to appear on the field. They filtered out of the dugout, paired off, and began to throw baseballs back and forth. As more appeared they took places closer to the left field bullpen. Someone with a bat began to tap easy grounders to a group of players who fielded the ball and then returned it. Jim Fregosi dropped a square white base marker on the grass and began to practice pivoting movements for the double play. Bobby Knoop joined him; together they scooped in grounders, tagged the base, and then simulated the throw to first.

Tom Satriano appeared beside Tibbs at the end of the tunnel. "How does it look?" he asked.

"It's perfect," Virgil said. "This is wonderful cooperation, especially after you've already played a full game."

"The boys will keep it up as long as you need them. I only hope it works."

"If nothing else it will certainly calm the boy down, give him something that he's intensely interested in to take his mind off his troubles."

"Do you think he'll come down?"

Tibbs shook his head. "I don't know. If the California Angels can't distract him, then it's hopeless. Do they know he has a gun?"

"Yes."

Virgil locked his fingers together and looked at them for a moment. "I know how valuable every one of you is to the team," he said slowly. "And if Minnesota loses today, you'll be in second place."

"They did and we are."

"I've got to admit an element of risk, but even in a crazed frame of mind, I can't believe that Johnny would take a shot at any member of the team; you're his one great interest in life."

"The guys understand that. Do you need me any

187

more? I'm supposed to speak at a dinner tonight in Los Angeles, but if you need me, I'll stay."

"You've done all that I could ask of you — and more," Virgil answered. "Keep your engagement by all means."

"In a way I hate to go," Satriano said.

"You have to, that's clear; I'm sure we'll be all right now."

On the field the fungo batter hit a sharp grounder which smoked across the grass. Bobby Knoop made a dive for the ball, snared it with his bare hand, and threw while he was still prone on his back. From up above, fragile in the air, a thin boyish voice gave a faint cheer.

It was the first encouraging sign. On the field there was a visible reaction; the players who had been going through the familiar warm-up routine began to snap the ball a little harder. The hitter popped the ball high into the air; an outfielder ran back and made a carefully calculated circus catch with a roll on the ground for a finish. In the very atmosphere around him Virgil was aware that all this was succeeding; that Johnny McGuire knew that his heroes were putting on a special show just for his benefit.

When Ted Bowsfield appeared at the end of the tunnel, Virgil turned to him with relief strongly written on his features. "In a few minutes, perhaps one or two of the men might wave to Johnny and invite him to join them. I think now that will make him come down. He'll feel that he's wanted, and that will give him his excuse."

"I'll arrange it right away," Bowsfield said.

"Don't bother," the slurred voice of Charles Dempsey cut in. The narrow youth had materialized from somewhere. "I'll pass th' word." Before anyone could grab him he ran out onto the field. He put his long legs to work and bolted out onto the grass like a dark streak. At long last he had a role to play and he was apparently determined to make the most of it. In his frustrated fury Virgil could have shot him.

Sport stopped to talk to the first two players he was able to intercept. Then he ran to the next group; there was no point in stopping him now. He was in full view; Tibbs's only hope was that the high angle involved would prevent him from being recognized from up above.

Then, when he had finished delivering his message for the second time, Dempsey yielded to the temptation to look up at the car from his new vantage point.

Nothing happened for a second or two, then from up on the high frame there came a startled, almost explosive noise edged with sudden acute desperation. There was pure anguish in it, like the cry of a wounded animal. It froze in the air as the car once more began to climb slowly, still higher up the steep framework.

"Cut the power!" Virgil barked, rage in his voice. Bowsfield signaled down the tunnel; moments later the car came to a halt.

"Now what?" the Angel executive asked.

If a grown man could cry, Virgil was in the mood.

"We've got a fire truck standing by," Bowsfield continued. "Three different men have volunteered to go up after him; they all know about the gun. I'm not sure, though — I think he's beyond the reach of the ladders now."

Tibbs watched dully as Dempsey hurried off the field, remorse now written on his face. On the outfield grass the baseball action continued, but it was mechanical now; every man there understood completely what had happened. They didn't know who Dempsey was, but they were acutely aware that his appearance had shattered the mood they had been working so hard to establish. The baseballs continued to travel back and forth, but they arced through the air as though they themselves had suddenly become dead and inert.

Virgil knew that it was now up to him; the one thing he could not do was give up. He would have to think of something and it would have to be good; Dempsey's sudden appearance had made matters even worse, if possible, than they had been when the desperately frightened boy had first taken refuge on the heights of the massive A-frame.

He had gone even higher now. He could not come down; the power was off and Virgil did not dare to have it turned on again. Not with the maintenance car able to make the dizzying circle suspended underneath the halo, the highest structure in Orange County. A cool-headed mechanic unafraid of heights could ride it, but it could paralyze an already fearfully upset nine-year-old boy. A boy equipped with a gun which, in a moment of total desperation, he might turn on himself.

Tibbs began to search all of the data he had accumulated for some ray of light — something to help him. And it would have to be soon, Johnny McGuire would not remain static too much longer. He had no way of reading what thoughts and fears might be running through the boy's mind, goading him on to some final act of horror.

Then it came to him. Almost calmly he turned to Ted Bowsfield and said, "I need your help."

"Name it," Bowsfield responded.

Virgil did — in four quick, condensed sentences. The Angel executive gave him a hard stare for a moment. "It just might work," he conceded. "Let's go."

He led the way briskly into the tunnel, pulling out a ring of keys as he did so. It was only a short distance to where the golf carts were parked; he slipped quickly into the nearest one and fitted a key into the lock. As soon as Virgil was beside him he pressed the pedal and the fully charged cart took off with considerable speed down the length of the bare concrete tunnel.

They ran rapidly past the clubhouse area and then onto a ramp which led upward. At the top Bowsfield executed a sharp U-turn and bit into another ramp which continued the rise.

"How far can you go in this thing?" Tibbs asked.

"All over the stadium, to any level. It's designed that way."

The ramp doubled back on itself; Bowsfield swung the cart around almost without slowing down and then was climbing again. The grind of the electric motor echoed through the ramp area; to the left the parking lot began to stretch out like a vast asphalt billiard table.

The cart ran onto the second level and began to scurry past the closed concession stands. Then another ramp appeared, Bowsfield steered onto it, and they were going up once more.

They came out this time onto a level where the view of the field was blocked by a solid concrete wall. "The ramp design was Cedric Tallis's idea when he was with us," Bowsfield commented. "It's a great help now."

They ran along the length of the concrete wall for a hundred feet and then Bowsfield brought the golf cart to an abrupt stop. The Angel executive fitted a key into a closed door at the end of the wall and without ceremony led the way through. As Tibbs followed he saw that they were high above the playing field now in the private box section reserved for the top personnel. A number of people were there: executives, secretaries, and service employees — all silently watching the drama being played out on the field. One careful look toward the scoreboard told Vigil that the situation had not visibly changed since he had left the area less than five minutes before.

The baseball action was still going on: a handful of gray uniforms were now mixed in as the Detroit players added their contribution to the effort. Up on the vaulting framework above the scoreboard the tiny car was visible just where it had been. Angrily Tibbs reminded himself that it could not have moved, he had ordered the power cut off.

Bowsfield touched him on the shoulder; he turned to find himself facing a firmly built man whose face he instantly recognized. "This is Virgil Tibbs," Ted said quickly and then completed the introduction. "Gene Autry."

As soon as the two men had shaken hands Tibbs took the floor. "Mr. Autry, some time ago at a personal appearance you spent a moment with that boy up there on the sign. You've been his hero ever since, and he trusts you completely. Will you help?"

"In any way that I can."

"Sir, by any chance do you have any of your cowboy regalia here at the stadium, anything at all? Even a ten-gallon hat?"

The owner of the Angels studied him for a moment. "I haven't made pictures for years," he said.

"You forget television, sir. Johnny McGuire, the boy up there, has seen you repeatedly. To him you're the greatest cowboy who ever lived." Virgil drew breath. "That goes for both of us," he added.

Gene Autry understood, he picked up a telephone which sat on the counter of the private box. "Get me Disneyland," he directed.

Tibbs stood silently beside Ted Bowsfield while the connection was made, and the call put through to the administrative offices at the amusement park.

"This is Gene Autry, at the stadium. I need something and I need it fast. I want a horse sent over here, fully saddled and ready to ride. A chestnut with a white blaze if you can do it, one that might pass for Champion."

He listened a moment.

"That's right, I don't care who you have to take it away from, this is an emergency and a big one. Please get that horse over here on the double. One more thing — don't come in the back way. Bring it in through the front gate, it'll be open and someone will be waiting for you. No more than fifteen minutes at the outside, never mind what it costs."

He hung up. "They'll do it," he said, then he looked at Tibbs. "Do you think that this is going to work?"

"When you met that boy," Virgil answered, "you called him your pal. He's an underprivileged lad; to him that was next to the voice of God."

"I used to sing a song that might apply here," Autry said. He led the way out of the executive boxes and across the aisle to the office area.

" 'Back in the Saddle Again,' " Tibbs supplied.

Autry looked at him. "You remember?"

"I was a boy too, sir; not too long ago. A Negro boy in the deep South, but that didn't make any difference."

The Angel owner led the way into his office suite. Then he slipped out of his coat and dropped it across a chair. He opened a closet door and reached in for a replacement. "Years ago," he said, "a boy was sick in a hospital. It was in

194

Boston as I remember. He asked for me and I went out to see him — in a business suit. He took one look and burst out crying. Then he said that I wasn't Gene Autry because Gene Autry was a cowboy. I didn't look the part. I learned something that day; now I'm prepared."

"Suppose we wait outside," Virgil suggested.

Eight minutes later Gene Autry, the heels of his cowboy boots clicking on the hard concrete, joined them. Virgil Tibbs took one careful look at him and his heart lifted; if this wasn't the answer, then he doubted if one existed on the face of the earth. "I've just lost twenty years," he said.

Autry gave him a shrewd look. "You may not be the best detective that Pasadena has," he commented, "although I suspect that you are. But you're a hell of a good psychologist. Let's go."

Ted Bowsfield drove the golf cart down the ramps with Gene Autry beside him and Virgil hanging on the back. When they reached the foyer area the horse had not yet appeared; they dismounted from the vehicle and reconciled themselves to an unavoidable delay.

Virgil turned to one of the several waiting ushers. "Any change?" he asked.

"No, sir, nothing we can see."

At that precise moment inspiration hit Tibbs. "Is the organist for the stadium still here by any chance?" he asked Ted.

"I think he is, do you want him?"

"Yes."

Bowsfield nodded and the usher took off in the golf cart. There was still no sign of the horse from Disneyland or any guarantee that one had been dispatched. Gene Autry was turning toward the lobby telephones when a girl came hurrying out from the office there. "Your horse is on the way, Mr. Autry," she reported. "It should be here in the next few minutes, if the traffic isn't too bad."

"It had better not be. Thank you." Autry replied.

The whine of the golf cart drew attention; it pulled up with the usher driving and a slender man beside him. Virgil did not waste time asking for his identity. "Can you play 'Back in the Saddle Again'?" he inquired.

"In what key would you like it?" the organist responded.

"I'll leave that up to you. Now here's the plot — it's vitally important that that poor frantic boy out there be completely convinced who it is when he sees Mr. Autry appear. The right music would help a lot."

"I understood, leave it to me. Just give me a cue when to begin."

A squeal of rubber came from outside as a horse van drew up. "Who's the stage manager?" Autry asked.

"Virgil," Ted Bowsfield replied.

"Then let's go," Tibbs said. "All we need is time to get back where we were and to make sure that someone is still standing by that power switch. When it's time for the organ music I'll signal, you'll know. Ted, can we go now?"

A few seconds later, in the golf cart, they were making excellent time down the deserted wide aisle provided for the patrons, then they dived down a ramp and were back in the underground complex. At full speed the cart stirred up a considerable breeze as it plunged down the last long tunnel and came out once more close to the left field bullpen. Sergeant Wilson was waiting for them there.

"No one, absolutely no one, is to run out onto the field under any circumstances," Virgil directed. "Even if he has to be restrained by force. That includes the boy's father. If we get the boy down, we're still not entirely out of the woods. We've got to disarm him and keep him from bolting."

"Right," Wilson agreed.

Virgil looked up and saw the organist wave from the press box area. "It looks like we're all set. Ted, can you get the players in off the field? Just as though an inning had ended?"

"Of course."

"All right, let's get on with our little play." Tibbs locked his fingers together and squeezed them. "At least we've got a top star."

There was the whine of a golf cart and an usher appeared. "Mr. Autry wants to know how many shots the boy has fired."

"Four," Virgil answered immediately, then he looked at Bowsfield and amplified the statement. "One into a playmate's house, two when he was stopped in the street, one at your usher. Correction: not *at* your usher, he deliberately aimed at the ceiling. The nick the bullet made was four feet in front of where your man fell down and almost five feet to the left. Even an inexperienced child couldn't miss that badly in a confined space at very short range."

The stadium manager was visibly startled. "You see things, don't you," he commented.

"That's my business," Tibbs replied.

The usher departed with the desired information and instructions to deliver a message at the clubhouse. Moments later Bill Rigney, the Angel field manager, appeared at the top of the dugout and waved his arm. Immediately the mock baseball practice ceased; the players from both teams ran at a jog toward the bench and quickly filled up most of the available space. In the sinking sun of late afternoon the vast stadium seemed quite abruptly to become stagnant and still.

In the third base stands, close to the bullpen, Mike McGuire sat silently, a policeman beside him apparently only as a fellow spectator. There were still many people in and around the baseball park, but almost all of them were intentionally well out of sight. Far across the field the executive boxes were well filled, but at that distance the occupants were barely visible. Thousands upon thousands of empty silent seats looked out unseeing at the broad spread of grass, at the deserted base paths, and the inert pitcher's mound.

Then the organist began to play. He started very softly,

so much so that the first wisps of the music seemed to drift almost naturally across the now still playing area. Gradually it began to take a little more coherent form as it increased very slightly in volume and became clearer in context. What had been only a featureless type of improvisation began to take on a certain flavor which is associated only with the great American West. A snatch of "Ghost Riders in the Sky" echoed and was gone, a few seconds later there was a suggestion of "Red River Valley."

It was so artfully accomplished that Virgil found himself being swept up into the mood. Through a kind of alchemy the skill of the lone musician was transforming a busy corner of rapidly expanding, freeway-striped Orange County into a vast and lonely prairie; the bare ground around second base seemed almost to be waiting for the restless tumbleweeds to come rolling by, propelled by a warm summer wind.

The harmonies began to swell and a certain feeling of subdued triumph impregnated them, it was almost impossible to resist the spell that was being created. The long curved rows of tens of thousands of empty seats remained motionless and mute, but life was in the stadium now, a life that could be heard and almost felt.

Then, behind home plate where the umpires normally appeared, a single figure came into view. It was a long way from the extreme end of left field, but it could not be mistaken — it was a man on horseback. His face was all but hidden by his wide-brimmed Stetson. As he began to ride slowly forward the chaps he wore on his legs were outlined and the pattern of his brilliantly decorated shirt began to be visible.

With a lofty disdain of the sacred areas of the baseball diamond the fine horse lifted his forefeet elegantly and stepped across the pitcher's mound as though it were a mere slight hump on some vast and featureless grazing land. The music grew clearer, it began to reach for something without quite attaining it; then it tried again, came nearer to the elusive melody, and finally, in a burst of triumph, captured it. Proud of its conquest it swung into the introduction to "Back in the Saddle Again," now clear and bright.

The well-trained horse at an unshaken even pace walked across the wide dirt area at second base and reached the outfield grass. The musical introduction ended on a sustained note and then the well-known melody burst out in full flower. The horse paused on direction and stood in splendid silhouette while the song was finished. Then, when the organ swung into "Tumbling Tumbleweeds" the horse again came forward, broke into a slow gallop, and turned toward the left field bullpen area. Within a hundred feet of the gate it stopped when it was reined in. The rider on its back reached up and with a fine sweeping motion took off his hat.

And then from high above the stadium, from the tiny sanctuary which had crawled so far up on the soaring A-frame, there came an excited, bursting, joyful cry in the treble voice of a young boy, *"GENE AUTRY!!!"*

Gulping, Virgil turned and swung his arm down to indicate that the power was to be turned on. He found Charles Dempsey behind him, anxious to be heard. "I'm sorry fo' what I done," he said urgently.

"Don't do it again," Tibbs said with grim sharpness. He had no more time for Dempsey at that moment, the drama was nearing its climax.

"Hi, Johnny, how's my pal?" the famous voice called out.

There was no answer.

"Can't you say, 'Hi, Gene'?" the man on horseback called.

It came back down, joy mixed with fright and awe. "Hi, Gene!"

"I can't hear you, you're too high!" Autry lifted his left hand and cupped it behind his ear.

"One," Virgil began, counting the seconds, "two, three, four, five, six, se —" At that point the car began to descend. It came down slowly and steadily until it was close to the top of the scoreboard — then it stopped.

"That's better!" On the back of his splendid mount the cowboy rode at a gallop in as big a circle as the outfield would allow. Virgil Tibbs checked the position of Mike McGuire and saw that his attention was riveted on his boy, but that he was making no attempt to leave the place where he was sitting. Apparently he understood that he could help now only by keeping out of the way. When the short ride was finished, the man on horseback drew up, pulled a gun from the holster which hung at his hip and fired into the air.

The shot rang out with raw power.

"Come on," he coaxed. "Don't you remember me? Where's your cowboy greeting?"

Quickly Virgil looked aloft once more and saw the head and shoulders of the boy who had been transplanted into another, better, and happier world. He saw him reach down for his own gun, hold it in both hands, and then fire it overhead into the air.

"Five," Tibbs said aloud to himself.

"Attaboy, Johnny, you do remember me!" Autry reined up tightly on his horse; in answer the animal rose up on its hind legs and for a moment pawed the air with its front hoofs.

"How about Champion?" The rider drew his gun and fired overhead once more. "You aren't going to forget him, are you?"

With intense concentration Virgil watched the boy. He saw his gun, he saw his hands go up as he pointed the weapon toward the sky, and then he heard the sharp bark of sound as the last shot was fired.

He was weak in the knees, but he still had his job to do. He turned toward the lanky teen-ager who still stood, open-mouthed beside him, and laid a hand on his shoulder. "Charles Dempsey," he said. "You are under arrest for the murder of Willie Orthcutt."

15

When the morning at last came, it was bright and beautiful. A fresh wind had blown away every trace of smog so that the close-by mountains stood out in needle-sharp detail. Across the street from the Pasadena police station the little cluster of trees around the parking lot was crowned with a rich summer green. The windows were all open, inviting the warm pleasant air of the near perfect day to permeate through the otherwise spartan working areas.

Captain Carl Lindholm sat in his office chair, his elbows on his desk, while he contemplated the face of the quiet, well-dressed man who stood before him. "I know that you had a tough day yesterday, Virgil," he said, "but I think we need a wrap-up on it this morning if you don't mind."

"Yes, sir," Tibbs said.

"A couple of things first. One: you'll be glad to know that the three men who pulled that double header are in custody. They've all got records and there's no doubt about it."

"I heard, sir. Congratulations."

"Next, since Chief Addis moving up into the top spot the position of Assistant Chief has been open."

Virgil held out his hand. "Congratulations again, sir. I'm delighted and I know that everyone else will be too."

Lindholm stood up to accept the offered hand and the feelings which went with it. "You know what I think of you, Virgil. All I can say is that I hope you will be with us for a long, long time."

"I hope so too, sir."

The phone rang and Lindholm answered it. He gave a brief directive and then hung up. "The visitors are down in the lobby. Before they come up, are you sure of your ground?"

"Yes, sir, very sure."

"Are the civil rights loopholes all plugged?"

"Absolutely, sir. I was present when Sergeant Wilson of the Anaheim police informed Dempsey of his civil rights. He was advised again here. An attorney is with him now."

"Good. Now you'd better explain things to these people and clear up a few points. There's one or two I want to hear you on myself."

Five minutes later there was a fair gathering in the captain's office. Ralph Hotchkiss was there with his son Billy, now a very chastened young man. He sat still in the chair that had been assigned to him and looked straight forward.

Mike and Maggie McGuire were fiercely self-conscious; Mike expressed himself by rubbing his hands together and looking carefully at everything visible in the room. Maggie held her son Johnny tightly by the hand and wished devoutly that it was all over. She did not want anything explained to her, she only wanted to be safely at home with her boy.

In quiet dignity the parents of Willie Orthcutt sat a little stiffly in the two remaining chairs. They were simply dressed, he in a threadbare suit which had nonetheless been carefully brushed for the occasion, his wife in plain unrelieved black which surrounded her ample figure with as much grace as it could.

When everyone was comfortably seated, the captain took quiet command of the meeting. "I want to thank all of you for coming here this morning so that we can help to clear away certain serious misunderstandings which, directly or otherwise, concern you all." He turned toward the Orthcutts. "Let me begin by saying that I am very deeply sorry for the tragedy which came to your home."

"Thank you," Orthcutt answered simply.

"I sincerely hope that you may find a little comfort in learning the truth of what happened. If you wish to leave at any time, please feel completely free to do so; I have a car standing by that will take you home."

"You've been very good to us," Mrs. Orthcutt said.

205

Despite her grief she was in control of herself and Lindholm admired her for it.

"Now I'm going to let Mr. Tibbs explain to you what happened; I think it's very important that you understand this, even though it may be painful for Mr. and Mrs. Orthcutt. Part of a policeman's job is to see that the guilty are punished, another part is to see that, insofar as possible, the innocent are not." When he had finished he settled back into his chair and prepared to listen.

Virgil Tibbs looked at his audience with the air of a man who is prepared to speak, but only reluctantly. "I think the best way to approach this," he began, "is to give you a more or less running explanation of what occurred. After that, if you have any questions, I'll try to answer them for you.

"Some weeks ago Mr. and Mrs. McGuire moved here from Tennessee with their son. Mr. McGuire's employment and prospects where he was were both limited, so he made the decision to move his family out here in the expectation of a better opportunity."

He paused for a moment, as though he were considering which words would be the best for him to use.

"Like many other people, Mr. McGuire has a strong sense of self-sufficiency and, also like many others, he expressed his feelings in part by keeping a revolver in his home — loaded and ready for use. Specifically it was a Colt Chief's Special, which is a particularly dangerous weapon. Unfortunately, he kept it where a child had access to it, told his son where it was, and to some degree instructed him in its use.

"To do justice to Mr. McGuire, I must point out that in keeping this unregistered weapon as he did, despite the great danger that it represented, *he was entirely within the law*, at least so far."

Virgil stopped and waited, but Mike McGuire remained motionless and did not utter a sound.

"One of the real dangers of owning a gun is the incentive it provides to shoot it out with possible intruders — which is a quick and easy way to get killed. Most home owners are insured against burglary. If there is any shooting to be done, let us handle it — that's our job. Private citizens aren't asked to take such risks, and if you do, you can get into serious legal complications."

He realized that he was editorializing and stopped. For a moment he stood, head down, his lips pressed hard together. Then he recovered himself and picked up the threads of the discussion.

"Two days ago Johnny McGuire took his small transistor radio to school. During the lunch hour it was snatched away from him and he was cruelly teased by Billy Hotchkiss. The end result was that the radio, which meant a great deal to Johnny, was broken in the scuffling. It was accidental and to his credit Billy offered to replace it immediately, but the fact remains that he was merciless in picking on someone younger and smaller than himself. For that he must stand responsible."

He looked at Ralph Hotchkiss, who nodded and indicated that he wanted to speak. "What you have just said is true and justified," he acknowledged. "Billy is still very young, but he certainly should have known better. I'm sorry that I didn't teach him better manners. For his inexcusable conduct I'd like to apologize now, publicly, to Mr. and Mrs. McGuire, and particularly to Johnny."

Without yielding to the temptation to do so openly, Tibbs watched the effect of Hotchkiss's statement on Mike McGuire. The proud man from Tennessee would have found such an open declaration impossible, he would have considered it humiliating. But on his face now there was an awareness that Hotchkiss had gained stature instead of losing it. The habits and attitudes of a lifetime were battling against the hard lessons he had learned during the past twenty-four hours; conciliation came very hard to him.

He made an effort, struggled, and succeeded. "I'll pay for the window Johnny broke," he said, "and for whatever else he busted."

Ralph Hotchkiss was no fool; he knew as well as Virgil did how hard that speech had been for Mike McGuire to make. He brushed his hand through the air to indicate that it was no matter. "I don't think you'll have to," he said. "The insurance company has already replaced the window and the rest was negligible."

Mike was relieved that he had been able to do the right thing without it costing him any money. "I'm to blame for what you went through," he added. "And Maggie and me, we're sorry."

Anxiously Maggie nodded to indicate her agreement.

Ralph Hotchkiss accepted gracefully. "Let's call it even," he proposed, and then turned back toward Tibbs, who was patiently waiting for this side discussion to end. When the room was again quiet, he continued.

"As you know, Johnny put a bullet through the Hotchkiss home and then fled. This was both a tort and a violation of the law. In view of Johnny's youth, and the state of mind he was in, Captain Lindholm has agreed to dismiss the matter from a police standpoint. So that much is now a closed incident unless Mr. Hotchkiss wishes to press charges."

Virgil did not even bother to look at Ralph Hotchkiss to see him shaking his head negatively.

"Thank you," Mike said to the captain, who nodded in reply.

"Johnny made his escape by city bus," Virgil continued, "and got off when he sensed that he was reaching the end of the line. At that point, I'm sure, he very much wanted to go home, but he was afraid to do so. He did not understand that any police officer would have helped him and protected him from harm. Considering what he had been taught, and what he had just done, his failure to ask a policeman for help is understandable, but it would far and away have been the best thing he could have done."

"Yes, sir," Johnny said.

Tibbs acknowledeged the remark. "You all know what happened after that — at least in part. Following the shooting, Johnny took refuge in Arroyo Seco Park and stayed there all night. It was unnecessary, because I was already almost certain, despite the evidence to the contrary, that he had not been responsible for the death of Willie Orthcutt."

That announcement had a decided effect, a wave of surprise went quickly through the room.

"As soon as I heard about the shooting, I went to the hospital where I found Charles Dempsey in the corridor. He gave me his account of what happened, a story which contained a glaring inconsistency. He told me that he had tried to disarm Johnny by seizing his arms unexpectedly from the rear. Now Dempsey is eighteen years old and has the reputation for being smart and alert. It is an idiotic thing to seize a person with a gun that way, *but it was incredible that he would do so with a close friend standing directly in front in the line of fire.* I will agree that people sometimes become excited and do very illogical things, but that was a more or less deliberate action which has been confirmed by an honest witness.

"Secondly, Dempsey insisted that two shots had been fired; that too I found very hard to believe. By his statement the first bullet had struck the victim in the abdomen, he had clasped his hands across his middle, and had sunk to the ground. Then, Dempsey claimed, Johnny fired a second shot almost immediately at the same target. That kind of act I simply couldn't associate with a badly frightened nine-year-old boy, especially one who took to his heels and fled the first moment that he could.

"A thirty-eight revolver has a considerable kick to it and makes a very loud noise. After firing once the boy would have been frightened half out of his wits, even though the shot might have been accidental. His subsequent conduct proves that. Also, if the initial shot were unintended, then a second deliberate one right behind it was all but out of the question. So I had very serious doubts about Charles Dempsey right there."

To Virgil's discomfort he found that Mike McGuire was staring at him as though he could not believe that this quiet, dark-skinned man had the ability to analyze human reactions. Actually, Mike was astounded that *any* policeman possessed more than normal intelligence.

"At this point," Virgil continued, "I had grounds for suspicion but nothing more. I could not prove that the gun had been accidently fired, I only believed this to be the case. My opinion was reinforced by the fact that Johnny was standing alone with four people he believed to be hostile to him literally surrounding him; one was in front, one on each side, and one behind him. Under these circumstances, despite the frame of mind he was in and his youth, he would know that if he were deliberately to shoot the boy in front of him, the others would jump him immediately. And he would have good cause to fear what they might do to him.

"Now let me return to Dempsey, the boy known as Sport. After we received the tragic news that Willie Orthcutt had succumbed, he put on a great show of grief. He even stated that he was going to find the boy with the gun and kill him. At that point I deliberately told him that the boy wasn't guilty, in those words. At once his whole manner changed, he dropped his pose and with almost animal intensity asked, '*Then who is?*' It was very clear that at that moment he was badly frightened."

"No wonder," Ralph Hotchkiss commented.

"I must point out again," Tibbs continued, "that all this was a very long way from legal evidence — it was only a guideline. Furthermore, there was a serious objection to Dempsey's guilt at that time and another appeared when I learned that Willie had been shot in the arm. When the hospital gave me that information, it created a major road-block."

He stopped and turned toward the parents of the dead boy. "Is this too painful for you?" he asked.

"No, sir," Orthcutt replied, his voice even and controlled. "We want to know what happened."

"At first I entertained the idea that Dempsey, for a motive not yet known, had brought about his supposed friend's death by placing his own hands over Johnny's and forcing him to shoot as he wished. After an experiment here in my office I convinced myself that this was not possible. I was forced to reexamine the matter and the exact nature of the wound in Willie's upper arm gave rise to some thought. Mr. Hotchkiss, would you be kind enough to stand up for a moment?"

Ralph Hotchkiss rose to his feet, not sure what to expect.

"I'd like you to assume, sir," Virgil said, "that you have just been shot in the left upper arm from directly in front of you." He reached out and touched the spot on Hotchkiss's arm where the supposed bullet had entered. "Now what do you do?"

In response Hotchkiss clapped his right hand over the area.

"That's what everyone does when they're suddenly hurt, they put their hand or hands over the place where the pain is. Now if you will look, sir, you will see that you have both forearms over your upper abdomen."

There was a silent tableau for a few seconds; Ralph Hotchkiss standing with his arms folded across his body, understanding dawning on his face.

"Three different people told me that Willie Orthcutt went down with his hands across his abdomen," Virgil explained. "If that were true, then it was apparently established that that was where he had been shot. But when I began to think a little harder about the wound in his upper arm, the light dawned and a second explanation for the arms across the body became permissible. Since the victim was a fourteen-year-old boy, it was understandable why he had sunk to the ground in pain, compounded by shock. I doubt if any one of us would, if we were unexpectedly shot, remain on our feet."

"When I checked on Charles Dempsey's background, I learned that he had once been arrested for armed robbery. Later he proved an alibi and was released, the charge was dismissed. I mention this only because it suggested to me that he might have had a gun; an innocent person without one would not likely have been brought in and booked."

At that moment Mike McGuire looked acutely uncomfortable; that hazard of owning a firearm had not occurred to him.

"Perhaps even more to the point was the way in which he behaved himself after Willie was hit. The only possible thing to do for a person who has been shot in the abdomen is to call an ambulance. I'm sure that Billy here knows that someone in that condition should not be moved except by qualified people who have the proper equipment, and Dempsey is far older and more mature. Yet he insisted on picking up the victim himself, refused offers of aid, and took him to the hospital in his own car. That too was incredible conduct; even if he had been greatly upset, he still would have known better."

He stopped and waited for a moment. The quiet in the room was thick now, even the fresh air flowing in the open windows could not dispel the specter of cold and terrible murder. Outside there were the sounds of cars and of people about, but those in the office ignored this evidence of life going on.

When he continued, Virgil's voice was quiet, but it carried the tone of final authority which would not be denied. "Now we come to the key point, the unshakable proof, of Dempsey's guilt. The gun with which Johnny McGuire was armed was, as I told you, a Colt .38 Chief's Special. It is a fairly common weapon which can easily be bought on the open market. It is lighter than some other guns, more compact, *and it holds only five shots.*

"Naturally I was keeping track of the number of bullets fired from Johnny's gun, because the fifth would be the last, if he fired that many, and the great danger that he represented to himself as well as to others would be over. His first shot went into the Hotchkiss house. Then, presumably, two more were fired at Willie Orthcutt. One in the stadium tunnel at Anaheim made four. The fifth shot was discharged into the air in answer to a salute fired with great presence of mind by Mr. Gene Autry who, I am now sure, deserves his enduring fame as America's greatest cowboy. That made five. Then Mr. Autry coaxed Johnny to fire once more; when he did *that made six shots from his gun which was impossible without reloading.* At that point I was immediately certain of two things: that Johnny had accidently shot Willie Orthcutt only in the arm and that Charles Dempsey, known to his associates as Sport, was Willie's murderer.

"Dempsey tried to convince me that Johnny had fired twice at young Orthcutt and so did one of his friends, but the other witnesses denied the second shot or were unsure. But it no longer mattered, Johnny had no way of reloading his gun and that fact in itself will convict Dempsey. Somewhere en route to the hospital, probably on a detour made for the purpose, Dempsey shot Willie Orthcutt in the abdomen, using his own gun. The bullet did not lodge in the boy's body and no ballistic tests were possible. I realize now that I should have taken Dempsey in that night for a paraffin test to determine if he had recently fired a gun, but I had at that time only a strong suspicion to go on and I was anxious to keep it to myself."

Outside the sounds of life going on seemed to be gaining in intensity. There were the noises of people and of voices, of cars and trucks passing by, and the subdued drone of a private plane overhead. Mrs. Orthcutt dabbed at the corners of her eyes with a small white handkerchief. She looked up and in a tone which betrayed her deep emotion spoke only one word. "Why?"

Virgil locked his fingers together, pressed them tightly, and seemed to gather himself together. "I want you to know," he said, "that this is almost as hard for me to put into words as it is for you to hear. Dempsey's motive was perhaps the worst thing of all; it occurred to me quite early, but I found it hard to believe. Later on, when I was having some difficulty with a militant individual, he made a grandstand play of a type which partially confirmed it. His hasty long trip to Anaheim to be in on what might well have been the finish of Johnny McGuire made my impression stronger still.

"I should not say this publicly, but you are entitled

to know: we have a confession. Following his arrest Dempsey knew that he was finished. He was carefully informed of all of his constitutional rights and told that he would have to stand trial as an adult, but he did not seem to care. He gave us the whole story and there is no longer any need for conjecture.

"Your son Willie, by all accounts including Dempsey's own, was an outstanding and talented boy. Dempsey stated that 'he had it all.' Willie was a handsome boy, he had definite musical gifts, and he was a natural leader."

Bob Nakamura appeared quietly in the door of the office and caught the captain's attention. He nodded toward the window. Lindholm turned halfway around in his chair, rose to his feet, and looked down at the street. Then he nodded silently to Nakamura, who disappeared. This bit of activity concluded he sat down again and turned back toward Tibbs, inviting him to continue.

"Willie's popularity was growing very rapidly, particularly as he was passing from boyhood into young manhood. Dempsey, more than any other thing, valued his status as the big man in his neighborhood among the Negro teenagers. He remarked on this several times in my presence, he even assured me that if I needed any help, he could supply it. He did, as it worked out, prove to be very valuable at one point, but his real purpose was to attract attention to himself and, of course, to divert any possible suspicions I might have. He had had quite a start in the hospital corridor and he wanted very much to be on safe ground, something which was, of course, impossible for him.

"He knew, however, as he has admitted, that his own endowments did not approach Willie's. Every report I have had on the dead boy stressed his potential: he was reported to be good-looking, smart, a talented musician, articulate, and destined for real success. This came to me on several occasions. Now compare this with Dempsey's own capabilities. His speech reveals that he was a poor student in school; he was, in fact, an early dropout. He can hardly be described as handsome and his prospects, even before the shooting, were very limited. Yet he stressed the fact to me several times that he was the 'big man' in his neighborhood. He did that in my office in the presence of the girl Luella.

"I would have had to be practically blind not to have noticed that with Willie alive, Dempsey's position of leadership was being severely threatened. In another year or two he would have no chance whatever against Willie Orthcutt — car or no car. He knew it, and it was a prospect he could not endure. That same motivation has, unfortunately, caused a great many political assassinations, perhaps even more than are recorded in history.

"Another factor, which I'm sure intensified Dempsey's desire to get rid of Willie at any cost, was Luella, the girl whom I referred to a moment ago. She is a very attractive teen-ager, who was described to me, before I met her, as more or less Charles Dempsey's girl, but my informant added that she also accepted dates with other members of Dempsey's clique. When I met this young lady it was immediately obvious that her mental and educational levels were superior to Dempsey's. Her speech very clearly revealed that. I also had an indication that Willie Orthcutt was interested in her. I don't attempt to forecast love affairs, but it was patently obvious that within a short time Dempsey's shortcomings as opposed to Willie's rising capabilities would become very obvious to Luella. Being a better educated girl herself, it was inevitable.

"Dempsey swears, and I tend to believe him on this point, that he never intended to do what he did, but when the opportunity was almost literally thrust upon him, with a once-in-a-lifetime chance to have someone else take the blame, his jealousy drove him to it. With Willie Orthcutt out of the way his position of leadership would be once more firm, and Luella would not be tempted away by someone better than himself. That motivation, incidentally, has also appeared before. He was unable to resist the temptation when he had the means at hand, his own unregistered, loaded gun, in his car."

Slowly Willie's father got to his feet and helped his wife out of her chair. "I think we best go," he said to the captain. "Thank you for asking us." Then he turned to Mike McGuire. "You must feel better in your mind now."

When he heard those words, Mike felt perspiration on his forehead; he remembered acutely that whatever else had happened, Johnny *had* shot this man's son — and with a gun he himself had virtually placed into his hands. As the captain picked up his phone, Mike steeled himself and held out his hand to the man his boy had wronged. Gravely the two men shook.

Unconsciously Mike wiped his palm on the side of his trouser leg after making his gesture, but it apparently passed unnoticed. The captain spoke and hung up; seconds later a uniformed officer arrived to escort the parents of the murdered boy home. "Use my car," the captain directed. "Take them out the rear way, it will be shorter and easier for them."

The policeman nodded his understanding. "Yes, sir, if they don't mind using the back door."

When the Orthcutts had gone Ralph Hotchkiss stood up. "In a way," he said to the captain and to Tibbs, "this whole series of events is at least partly our responsibility, and I'm very aware of it. I can assure you that nothing like it will ever happen again, at least not where Billy is concerned. We're going to go now and get Johnny a new radio." He turned toward Mike. "We'll be over later this afternoon to deliver it if you'll be home."

Mike nodded silently, not knowing what to say. For the first time in his adult life he felt the inadequacy of his own powers of speech. Silently he shook hands with Hotchkiss and watched the father and son as they left the office. Then he turned to the captain. "Thanks for what you did for us," he said stiffly. He reached into his pocket, extracted his handgun, and laid it on the desk. "Here, you can have it," he said. "I don't want the damn thing any more."

"It's your property, sir," Lindholm answered, ignoring the technicality that it was legally a concealed weapon. "If you'd like, we'll be glad to register it for you for your protection."

Mike shook his head. "You keep it." He left it at that.

Captain Lindholm directed his attention toward Johnny. "I never did hear how you finally came down off that sign," he said.

"Mr. Autry told me to and I did," Johnny answered. "Then he gave me a ride on his horse. I sat right up there beside him on Champion."

"Johnny, are you ever going to do anything like this again?"

"No, sir!"

"Now, Johnny, I'm satisfied that you didn't intend to shoot your gun at the Orthcutt boy."

Johnny burst into tears. "I was scared."

"I'll accept that explanation, so you don't need to worry about it any more. Now you go out into the hallway and wait there; I want to speak to your father for a minute."

Obediently, Johnny did as directed. When he was out of earshot Captain Lindholm addressed himself to Mike. "Mr. McGuire, I realize that you have been through a great deal during the last two days, and Mrs. McGuire as well. Based on what Mr. Tibbs has told me about you, I am inclined to believe that you have undergone something of a change of heart concerning police officers and the public service which we are trying to render."

Mike swallowed hard, but remained still. His silence became an admission, and even in that form it was hard for him.

"I've looked into the matter of the traffic citation you have outstanding," the captain continued. "The other car concerned was damaged and either you or your insurance company will have to pay for all necessary repairs. Taking into account your welcome change of attitude toward us, and certain other considerations, I'm willing to reduce the charge from reckless driving to unsafe lane changing. That will save you a considerable amount on your fine; I suggest that you spend some of it to take your son to the ball game."

Mike swallowed hard, looked at his wife, and gained encouragement from what he saw written on her face. He drew breath, hesitated, and then forced himself to use a simple word for the first time in his life. "I will, sir," he said. "Thank you very much. I couldn't pay the big fine; we ain't got much."

"I understand. Where is your car parked, sir?"

"Across the street, in the lot."

"Then perhaps it would be well if I had one of my men pick it up and drive it around to the back for you. We have a disturbance out front at the moment and until we've dealt with it, I think it would be better if you didn't appear."

Virgil knew, before he looked, what to expect. He glanced out of the window and saw the picket line, the signs with his name on them, the leader, a tall black man in flamboyant African robes. This was not a mass demonstration, this was peaceful picketing, but it would be made up of hard-core militants.

"I'll take care of it," Tibbs said.

"It might be better not," the captain counseled. "They're after your hide. Larry Harnois is the man."

"Larry is damn good," Tibbs countered, "but this one is mine. It's a matter of complexion."

Lindholm did not tell him to be careful, or what to do. He watched as Tibbs walked out of his office, then he picked up the phone once more. He spoke to Larry Harnois and gave some specific directions.

Now that the meeting in the captain's office was over, Virgil found himself in a strangely calm frame of mind. The fact that fifty or sixty men were picketing the police headquarters, protesting his actions, did not disturb him in the least. Johnny McGuire had been safely restored to his parents, Dempsey was in custody, and the immediate crisis was over. The picketing was a nuisance, but he did not regard it as a dangerous one.

In complete possession of himself he walked through the small lobby, pushed open the front door, and started down the fifty odd feet of sidewalk which led to the curb.

The leader spotted him before he had gone five steps. He let out a yell and then spread his arms to indicate that his followers should fall in behind him.

Without slowing his pace Tibbs walked up to within

five feet of him and stopped. "You wanted to see me?" he said.

The man planted the palms of his hands on his hips and surveyed him with hard hostility. "You're the one who's betrayed his people," he accused loudly enough for all to hear.

"What people?" Virgil asked.

"Black people!"

"Is that all you can say for yourself — that you're black?" Tibbs retorted.

He shook a powerful fist under Tibbs's nose. "Don't you get fresh with *me*!" he challenged. "You know what I can do."

Tibbs took in the black faces and realized that these were the hard types; nothing he could say or do would have any influence on them.

"Where's that goddamned white boy that shot my soul brother?"

"The man who murdered him is in jail right there." He pointed casually toward the fourth floor. "And get this in case it means anything to you — he isn't white."

There was a protesting roar; the pickets pressed closer now and out of the wave of sound words like "fake" and "frame-up" emerged with ugly edges.

The leader filled his powerful lungs. "I'm going to rip you to pieces. I'm going to make you crawl in the dust and beg for mercy from the black people you've betrayed. I'm going to make you hate the day you were born!"

"No you're not. You've had your say and that's enough. Now I'm going to tell you what black power is."

The speaker seized the opportunity to ridicule him. "Be real quiet, boys, he's goin' to tell us what black power is. He's goin' to tell me the meaning of black power. He's goin' to turn the tide of Black America; he's goin' to stop us from taking over the country. This black boy with the brown nose!" He swept his arms wide so that the brilliant colors of his African robes dominated the scene.

"You're a phoney," Tibbs said. "And you're a poor excuse for a black man. All you can do is make a loud noise and then sit in courtrooms reading the thoughts of Mao Tse-tung while you're waiting to be tried. And you look like a freak."

"Are you calling me a freak!"

"You're damn right I am," Virgil shot back. He did not yell like his opponent, but his words carried an even greater power. "You aren't a leader, you couldn't shine Ralph Bunche's shoes."

For a moment it seemed as if Tibbs might be losing control of himself. His face was contorted now and unconsciously he had doubled his hands into fists.

"Get it through your head that I'm a black man. And I've been one a lot longer than you. That means that things were that much tougher when I grew up and got shoved off the sidewalk by young white punks who thought they owned the world."

225

The militant tried to wave him down, but Tibbs would not be stopped. "I know more about being a Negro than you ever will, because I fought for the right to live in the South before civil rights was in the dictionary."

With his right arm he elbowed the bigger man aside almost as though he were not there. When he continued a fire of urgency burned in his words, and total intensity had seized the features of his face.

"I heard about Booker Washington and George W. Carver and then like a kid I dreamed that some day a great man would come, with a black skin, that the whole world would look up to and honor."

"And when we looked there was Martin Luther King. Nobody shoved him aside when he stood up to accept the Nobel Prize, but some bastard couldn't stand it, so he shot him. And while things like you cried for black power and started riots that ripped apart the Negro sections in Newark and Detroit other men stood up to take his place."

He stopped suddenly, his teeth clamped hard together. Then he consciously regained control of himself; when he spoke again it was almost calmly. "I work here because nobody cares whether I'm black or white, just so long as I do my job. I clawed my way up against prejudice, I licked poverty, and I earned my job. And here I'm not a black man, I'm Virgil Tibbs, a respected police officer, and nobody asks for anything more. I just caught a murderer who's in a cell upstairs. Now who the hell are you!"

He had nothing more to say after that. He knew that he could not change the jeering mob of professional militants, but he could show that he was not afraid. He knew that he had done that.

He turned on his heel and outwardly as calm as he had been when he had come out, he walked back into the aging building which houses the headquarters of the Pasadena police.